D1082811

CORRIGAN AND THE TOMB OF OPI

Corrigan opened the door

CORRIGAN AND THE TOMB OF OPI

by

R. B. MADDOCK

Illustrated by Robert Hodgson

THOMAS NELSON AND SONS LTD
LONDON EDINBURGH PARIS MELBOURNE
TORONTO AND NEW YORK

THOMAS NELSON AND SONS LTD

Parkside Works Edinburgh 9
36 Park Street London W1
312 Flinders Street Melbourne C1

302–304 Barclays Bank Building
Commissioner and Kruis Streets
Johannesburg

THOMAS NELSON AND SONS (CANADA) LTD
91–93 Wellington Street West   Toronto 1

THOMAS NELSON AND SONS
19 East 47th Street New York 17

SOCIÉTÉ FRANÇAISE D'EDITIONS NELSON
25 rue Henri Barbusse Paris V^e

———

First published 1957

CONTENTS

LIST OF ILLUSTRATIONS

CHAPTER I

THE TOMB OF OPI

THE Oasis Hotel, Cairo, reared up above the palms which surrounded it and shone white in the cool Egyptian moonlight. Its windows glowed with life, and from it came Eastern spicy smells and the harshness of Western music.

Its dining-room, all chromium-plate, long mirrors and thick gentle carpets, was the eating-place of nations, where East met West in equal luxury. Shrimp Bradley was sitting at a corner table looking across the crowded room and listening to the motley buzz of Arabic, French, German, Russian and English. A cool draught came down from the big silent fans in the ceiling. He turned, smiling, to the man who was sitting with him.

'Talk about the United Nations!' he said quietly.

1

Geoff Oppenheimer was wondering how this small neat Englishman with the shy smile and friendly face managed to look so cool in the hot Egyptian night. He nodded. 'Gets you dizzy, I guess. Every colour of skin known to man and half his languages in this room tonight. Imagine the effect on *me*! I flew in only yesterday and this is my first trip outside the States. Mrs Oppenheimer's boy pitched straight into what sounds like a session of the United Nations! Not to mention the dust, flies and heat outside.' He looked at Shrimp. 'You should be okay, I guess. All the travelling you've done ought to have acclimatised you to this sort of thing.'

Shrimp liked the big-boned American with the close-cropped round head and the thoughtful little wrinkles at the corners of his eyes. 'I never get used to it,' he said. 'Never. Incidentally I haven't done so much travelling. I've been in Malaya, that's all.'

Geoff Oppenheimer had met Shrimp for the first time yesterday at this same table, Shrimp and the big guy, Corrigan. He knew that they worked in Malaya on a rubber estate and that they were now on their way back to England on leave. 'Where's your pal?' he asked.

Shrimp smiled again. 'Corrigan? He'll be here soon. Takes plenty of time over his bath does Corrigan.'

'Slow-moving, eh? Big men often are.'

'I wouldn't say that Corrigan's slow-moving,' Shrimp answered. He grinned. 'I know one or

two people who think lightning's slow compared
with Corrigan.'

' How come ? '

Shrimp stared thoughtfully across the room.
He wasn't seeing it. He was seeing the far-away
green jungles of Malaya with their gloomy dampness and their vast silences and sudden alarms.
' Corrigan has a great gift for getting into trouble,'
he explained quietly, ' and as a friend of ours once
said, he also has a genius for getting out of it. He
gives the impression of moving slowly, but, when
he needs to, he can move so quickly that it takes
your breath away. There are dacoits in Burma
and terrorists in Malaya who'll always regret that
they thought Corrigan slow-moving.'

Geoff ate slowly for a few moments and then
he nodded. ' Yeah, I know what you mean. You
can see it in those blue eyes of his. When he isn't
very pleased they have a way of going so cold you
hear the ice crackle. Not a good man to have on
the other side.' He looked up. ' You work with
him in Malaya ? '

' Yes. His uncle is a rubber-planter and we
both work on the estate. At the moment we're
on our way home to see what England looks
like in spring. It's two years since Corrigan last
saw it.'

' How come you're in Cairo ? '

' We broke our journey here. We're having a
few days to look round—you know, the Nile and
the Pyramids. The usual tourist things.'

Geoff smiled broadly and the thoughtful wrinkles

vanished so that he looked like a boy. ' Well, I certainly hope that your pal keeps out of trouble while he's here.'

Then Corrigan came walking between the tables towards them. People glanced up at the broad-shouldered young Englishman with the fair hair and the energy-saving walk. A Sudanese waiter, his polished black face wrinkling into a grin, was at his elbow as he sat down.

' Hello, you two,' said Corrigan. ' So you couldn't wait ? '

' I was starving,' Shrimp answered, ' and you can't expect a man to starve while you take a bath, Corrigan.'

Corrigan grinned at him. ' For a chap your size you have the biggest stomach in the animal kingdom.' He looked at the American. ' And how were the Pyramids ? ' he asked.

' Great ! Better than I'd hoped. No trippers. I'm going to spend a week among them. There are one or two inscriptions I want to decipher.'

Shrimp's eyebrows went up. ' Inscriptions ? You mean those hieroglyphs ? Don't tell me you can *read* that stuff ! '

Geoff rubbed the top of his bristly head self-consciously. ' I guess so. You see that's my subject —Egyptology.'

Shrimp looked worried. His idea of an Egyptologist was a stooping old man with a quavering voice, thick glasses and no hair. ' You mean mummies and tombs and so on—the real thing ? ' he asked unbelievingly.

Corrigan laughed suddenly. ' Shrimp's a botanist and he thinks that a man who's anything else isn't civilised. So that's your reason for coming to Egypt ? To study Egyptology.'

The American nodded energetically. ' Sure ! I just finished at the university. I'm an archaeologist, but my special interest is Ancient Egypt, and my father said he'd stake me to a trip out here and a stay of six months, to round off my studies.'

' Nice father ! ' Shrimp murmured.

Geoff smiled uncertainly. He felt uneasy in the presence of these two assured young men who earned their own livings and depended on nobody. ' Well, it's okay for him, you see. He's pretty well fixed—well off—and this gets me off his hands for six months. He thinks I'm nuts to go in for archaeology. Says the past's a waste of time and it's the future I ought to be interested in. He's spent his life in the canning industry. Any industry's a pain in the neck to me, but archaeology has always fascinated me.' His eyes were glowing with enthusiasm but suddenly the glow died and he looked embarrassed. ' I guess I talk too much.'

Shrimp's smile was full of understanding. ' Not you ! I think you're absolutely right to go all out for a job that interests you. Too many chaps take jobs their fathers like.'

' Let's go into the lounge for coffee,' Corrigan suggested. ' It's cooler and more comfortable.'

They sank into the comfort of the lounge. It was a big room, with cunning lighting and fly-nets over the windows to keep out the hungry mosquitoes from the Nile. It was a room of secret alcoves, potted palms and deep comfortable chairs, and it seemed to have been designed for confidential meetings.

Corrigan sipped his coffee and studied the American. He liked the clear brown eyes set in the thin face ; short-sighted eyes they were, which could screw themselves up in concentration or in friendly laughter. Now there was a shadow in them and the wrinkles at the corners of them pointed to it. Corrigan wondered. Worry, doubt, fear ? He did not know. He had seen that shadow several times ; seen it come and seen it go when its cause was momentarily forgotten.

'You were telling us,' he said, 'that you're here to study Egyptology. What exactly are you going to do ? '

The shadow went like magic and Geoff's eyes warmed up. 'The difficulty's going to be fitting everything in. That's why I started in right away today by going to the Pyramids. I could spend the six months there, going over the Pyramids and the tombs around them and the Sphinx. But I also want to spend a lot of time in the museum here in Cairo, and I must go south to Thebes and the Valley of the Kings. I reckon I'm going to be busy.'

Shrimp was watching Corrigan, watching him casually but carefully. He knew by the set of Corrigan's mouth, by the penetrating clearness of his eyes, by the alertness of his body that Corrigan was searching for something.

(1,824)

'It sounds pleasantly like a working holiday,' Corrigan was saying. He smiled. 'But I've an idea that you've missed out something. Maybe you don't want to tell us, but it might help if you did.'

The American, startled, glanced up quickly. He was looking straight into Corrigan's eyes and he could feel them probing and seeking. 'How do you mean?' he asked.

'I mean that I've a feeling that there's something at the back of all this you're keeping to yourself, and my bet is that it's something you're worried about.'

Geoff sank into his chair. He nodded. 'You're dead right. There is something. But it's so darned silly I don't like to talk about it.'

'We'll listen,' Corrigan said quietly.

Geoff sat and thought for a few seconds and stared at the rich carpet between his feet. Then he looked up at Corrigan and Shrimp. 'Ever hear of the lost Tomb of Opi?' he asked.

They shook their heads and he went on.

'Opi was the Chief Priest of Amun-Ré during the reign of Pharaoh Tuthmosis the Third, about 1500 B.C. That's something like three thousand five hundred years ago. He was also Grand Vizier of Upper and Lower Egypt. He was a big shot. He ruled the country when Tuthmosis was away on one of his military expeditions, which was pretty often. Tuthmosis Three was the Napoleon of Ancient Egypt. Opi prepared for himself a grand rock-cut tomb, just like all the big shots did. It took years to construct and when it was finished it was finer than all the others, finer even than Pharaoh's. Opi knew it was going to be. That's why he daren't have it anywhere near the royal necropolis.'

' The royal *what* ? ' Shrimp interrupted.

' Cemetery. The place they call the Valley of the Kings, across the Nile from Thebes. All the nobles tried to get their tombs as near as possible to the royal tombs. But not Opi. He daren't. He was afraid that if the Pharaoh saw his tomb he would be jealous. Even Chief Priests and Grand Viziers were scared of the Pharaoh. So Opi had his tomb made in the Jebel Ataka several hundred miles from Thebes.'

' And where and what might the Jebel what's-it be ? ' Shrimp asked.

' It's a range of mountains,' Geoff explained. ' *Jebel* means " mountains ". They overlook the Gulf of Suez at the northern tip of the Red Sea. I believe that they're wild and barren and absolutely uninhabited today, just as they were in Opi's time. That's why he chose to be buried there.' He looked at Corrigan and Shrimp and they could see the determination behind his little smile. ' I want to find that tomb,' he said.

' Why ? ' Corrigan asked.

' I don't want to spend all my time in Egypt doing the tourist routine or even doing what the average student does. I want to do something special and this is it—finding the Tomb of Opi.'

' Sounds as if you might be giving yourself

quite a job,' Corrigan said. ' Finding a tomb that's been lost for over three thousand years could be difficult.'

' It hasn't been lost all that time,' Geoff said. ' It was found at the end of the last century by a German, more or less by accident. It was empty, cleaned out by tomb robbers hundreds of years ago, like nearly all the tombs.'

Shrimp looked puzzled. ' But if it's been found, what's the idea of your trying to find it ? Or did this German lose it again ? '

' Correct ! He lost it again. He came across it, examined it briefly and left it. But he didn't record its exact location and nobody's been able to find it since. I told you it's in wild country.' Geoff smiled. ' I guess it isn't a very important tomb either, if it comes to that, so nobody looked very hard for it. There were plenty of other tombs which were more interesting so there's never been any real attempt to find it.'

' And why do *you* want to find it if it's so unimportant ? ' Corrigan asked.

Geoff shrugged. ' It hasn't been recorded, you see. I want to find it and copy, or photograph, the inscriptions and translate them. The Ancient Egyptians left a record of their lives—the complete story—on the walls of their tombs and these records are very interesting. From them we have obtained most of our knowledge of Ancient Egypt.' He smiled self-consciously and rubbed the top of his head again. ' Now if I could do this and maybe write a little book on it, it would help to establish me as an Egyptologist.' He leaned back and his eyes shone with anticipation. 'THE TOMB OF OPI : Its History and Importance, by Geoffrey Derringer Oppenheimer,' he whispered, and then he blushed and smiled. 'That's my full name. Stupid, isn't it ? '

Shrimp snorted. 'If you think yours is stupid, wait till you hear Corrigan's.'

'Why ? What is it ? '

'He'll kill me for this,' Shrimp answered with a giggle, 'but here goes ! Robert Delight Corrigan ! Now how do you like *that* for a monicker ? '

They turned to Corrigan, laughing, and saw that he wasn't listening. He was staring across the lounge, looking into a big mirror on the opposite wall and in it he could see the reflection of an Egyptian, a brown-skinned man of about thirty, with fat round cherub-cheeks and the dark deep eyes of a Pharaoh. The Egyptian was dressed in a light suit and he was standing amongst the palms behind Geoff, so tense and still and breathless that he must have been listening.

'Good evening, Mr Badri,' Corrigan said in a loud voice. 'You lost something ? '

The Egyptian jerked, and his face relaxed into a smile so pleasant and deferential that it was sickening. He walked out of the palms and stood before them.

'And what is the manager of the Oasis Hotel doing in this potted palm-grove ? ' Corrigan asked. 'Don't tell me he's seeing to the comfort of his guests.'

The Egyptian threw up his hands in exaggerated despair. ' But that is what I do, Mr Corrigan! I see that my guests come to the lounge, and that son of a lunatic I have for night porter he has not put on the fans. *Maknoon!* Is hot tonight, so I, Ahmed Badri, put them on. The switches, Mr Corrigan, are on the wall behind the palms.' For a second cunning flashed in his eyes.

Corrigan smiled and looked up at the big fans whirling silently in the ceiling. ' Nice of you, Mr Badri. It *is* hot, but I've known it worse.'

Ahmed Badri mopped his shining face. ' But this heat, Mr Corrigan! Is too much. Is hot and I die hourly! ' He turned to Geoff. ' I hear something you say, Mr Oppenheimer. You speak of the Tomb of Opi. Now I, Ahmed Badri, am interested in this tomb. Is impossible that I find it because I have much to do in this hotel. If you find it I beg that I may see it.'

Fox! Corrigan said to himself. He's heard everything we've said and he admits to hearing a part of it.

Geoff was sitting up, smiling. ' Sure! I'll be delighted to show you around—if I find it. I happen to know that you're quite an Egyptologist yourself so I'll be glad of your advice.'

Badri shrugged and smirked. ' I am the amateur, Mr Oppenheimer. Our great Egyptologist is Dr Goneim and I hear his lectures at the University. I have done some little work myself.'

Geoff nodded enthusiastically. ' I'll say you

have ! I read about your work at Sakkara. That was a highly skilled job, Mr Badri, and that's why I decided to stay at your hotel.'

The Egyptian bowed. 'Is too kind what you say. But it is not only my interest in Ancient Egypt which causes me to see this tomb. It is that I, Ahmed Badri, believe that Opi was an ancestor of mine.'

'No !' Geoff exploded incredulously. 'After three thousand five hundred years ? '

Badri's eyes narrowed. 'I believe it, Mr Oppenheimer. I do not ask that others should believe it also.' He smiled and wiped his glistening face. 'If I might suggest something, gentlemen ? It is hot and it is early yet. It is also the night of the full moon. Nobody should visit Cairo unless he sees the Pyramids in the moonlight. There it will be cool and beautiful. Will you not go ? '

'Say !' Geoff beamed. 'That's an idea ! How about it ? '

'Suits me,' Corrigan murmured, and Shrimp nodded.

Badri smiled and bowed low, and Corrigan wondered about the oiliness of the man and about his eyes, deep Eastern eyes flecked with mystery. 'I order the porter to bring your car, Mr Oppenheimer,' the Egyptian was saying as he left them.

'Your car !' Shrimp said. 'Does he mean that you have your own car out here ? '

Geoff gave a self-conscious nod. 'Yeah. Well, not really mine. I hired a Packard for the six months I shall be here. I'll have plenty of running around to do.' He smiled. ' I'll be happy to run you out to the Pyramids.' The enthusiasm was dawning in his eyes again. ' I'll bet they're quite a sight in the moonlight. I've heard that people go there for picnics at full moon. Nice of Badri to suggest it.'

' He's a queer fish,' Corrigan said quietly. ' It's only the second time I've spoken to him but he does something to me.'

' Me too,' Shrimp agreed. ' In my case he gives me the creeps. I know I creep easily, but he's so oily and smooth and—and villainous ! '

' He's okay,' Geoff said with a laugh. ' He's smooth because he has the smooth talk of a lot of these Egyptians, but he's okay. It's just that he's Egyptian.'

' It's just that he's queer,' Corrigan repeated, ' and it doesn't matter to me if he's a Red Indian or a Zulu. Some of my best friends have darker skins than his. What do you know about him ? '

Geoff shook his head. ' Not very much. He's supposed to be wealthy. He's well educated— went to Oxford or Cambridge or one of your universities—and he's made a bit of a name for himself as an Egyptologist.' He sat up. ' Shall we go ? The car should be at the front by now.'

Corrigan held up his hand. ' Hold on a minute. You hadn't finished what you were telling us when Badri butted in.'

Geoff looked puzzled. ' Hadn't finished ? I'd told you as much about the Tomb of Opi as I know.'

Corrigan nodded. 'Sure! But you hadn't told us about the thing that's worrying you.'

There was a pause while Corrigan and Shrimp watched him, and then Geoff leaned back in his chair and smiled. 'I hadn't, had I? It's too silly, but I'll tell you. When I got back to the hotel this evening at about six o'clock I found a note on the floor of my room. It had been pushed under the door.' He paused again.

'And what did it say?' Corrigan prompted him.

Geoff smiled again, self-consciously. 'That's the bit that's so ridiculous. I've torn it up but I can remember it. It went something like this: "Be warned by Opi that all who seek his eternal habitation must die." That's all.'

' "Eternal habitation"?' Shrimp muttered.

Geoff nodded. 'That's what the Ancient Egyptians called their tombs. You see, to them the tomb was a home for the soul for eternity. The soul lived there. That's why they took so much trouble with it and why it was so well furnished.'

Corrigan was thinking and muttering to himself. ' "Be warned by Opi". Almost as if the old boy had written it himself, and he's been dead for over three thousand years.' He looked up and grinned. 'I don't believe it, not after all that time. Imagine a priest of Ancient Egypt who could write English after being dead for so long. Somebody's trying to scare you off. Why?'

The American shook his cropped head in a puzzled way. 'Search me! There's nothing of

value in the tomb. It's absolutely empty—rifled—
according to the only report we've ever had on it.
So I don't get it.'

'And what are you going to do about it?'
Shrimp asked.

'Do? I'm going to have a good try at finding
that tomb. I've come too far to be put off by a
note under the door.'

Corrigan patted Geoff's shoulder. 'Good for
you! And if you find your tomb you'll also find
something else—why somebody doesn't want you
to find it. And that may be more interesting than
the tomb.' He thought for a moment. 'I wish
we could help you but we're due to catch a plane
for England in a few days, and we daren't miss it.'
He glanced out of the corner of his eye at Shrimp.
'Or dare we, atom?'

Shrimp was shaking his head firmly. 'No!
We're catching that plane! No more trouble!
We've had our share of trouble. We're on holiday.
Remember?'

Corrigan grinned. 'So that's it, Geoff. The
Tiny Tyrant here says we must go home, and he's
a mighty persistent tyrant.' He stood up. 'And
now what about those moonlit Pyramids?'

CHAPTER II

THE SHADOW OF THE PYRAMID

THE big Packard convertible was open. Geoff drove it swiftly and quietly through the tumult of the glaring Cairo streets, with their smells of coffee and of aniseed and their noisy jostle. Corrigan and Shrimp sat beside him on the bench seat. They watched the car's bonnet thread through the traffic and slide past the side-streets with their night shadows. Then quite suddenly the car was out of Cairo and going through Gizeh village and past Mena House, brightly lit in the moonlight, and already the desert was all round them in vast levels of unending sand which stretched away into the distance. They were in another world, an ancient, quiet, unreal world.

Geoff slid the big car up the Pyramid plateau and stopped it. For a few seconds nobody moved. They sat and looked. The Pyramids were pointing up towards the dimmed stars and throwing down great triangles of blackness on to the sand, and the Sphinx, softened by the moonlight, was gazing eastwards across the Nile Valley in its many-thousand-year guardianship of the tombs. The cool light hid the effects of time and vandalism ; the injured Sphinx-face, the torn-off casing of the Pyramids, the sand-blasted stone and the stupid scratched tourist initials were gone.   Old Egypt was reborn at full moon.

'We've slipped back a few thousand years,' Shrimp whispered.

The others nodded and they climbed out of the car, closing its doors quietly, unconsciously afraid of disturbing the ancient people who had worked hard here for their long rest.

Geoff began to walk and Corrigan and Shrimp followed him.   They walked along the northern side of the Great Pyramid for about half its length and there Geoff stopped.   They had the plateau to themselves.

'Wonderful night ! ' Corrigan murmured.

'Marvellous ! ' Shrimp agreed.   'And there's nobody here but us.   Not a soul for miles ! '

Geoff smiled.   'I wouldn't be so sure of that,' he said.

Corrigan and Shrimp looked at him, attracted by the thrill in his voice.   'How d'you mean ? ' Corrigan asked.

Geoff raised his left hand towards the bulk of the Pyramid.   'The Great Pyramid of Cheops,' he said.   The tomb of a king !   Thousands died building it ! '   He pointed with his right hand towards the clustered little pyramids, crumbling and broken, and the hundreds of robbed rectangular tombs.   'Pyramids and mastabas ! ' he went on. 'Hundreds of 'em !   Where hundreds of people, queens, princesses, nobles and officials were buried as near to their Pharaoh as they could get.'   He looked at Shrimp.   'And you say we have this

place to ourselves ! ' He gave a dry odd laugh.
' You say there isn't a soul for miles ! I guess the
place is stiff with souls—souls of men and women
and children who have been dead for thousands of
years and whose last homes are here all round us.'
He stopped and glanced over his shoulder. ' Listen !
Can't you hear them ? Can't you smell death ? '

Shrimp's shudder was cold. He pushed his
hands into his pockets and stood perfectly still. He
was still cold, cold and shivering in the darkness of
the pyramid-shadow. Some distance away the
desert lay white under the moon. It was smooth,
rounded and full.

Then Corrigan gave a snort of laughter and the
others looked at him. ' Any more of that stuff,
Geoff '—he grinned—' and you won't be smelling
death ; you'll be smelling my fist on the end of
your nose.'

Geoff was startled but soon began to smile his
embarrassment. ' Okay ! It was worth a try
anyway.'

' What was worth a try ? ' Shrimp asked, his
face puzzled and bewildered.

Geoff shrugged. ' I guess I was trying to throw
a scare into the pair of you. I thought as it was a
spooky night I'd invent a few spooks. It didn't
work.'

A sudden cold breeze from the east set the
fine sand trickling down the great stone blocks
and between them. Shrimp shivered again and
gasped. ' It did work, you know,' he whispered.
' Look ! '

They followed the direction of his trembling finger. Near to the north-western corner of the pyramid they could see the shadowy motionless figure of a man who had stepped clear of the darkness and into the moonlight. He was watching them. He was dressed in a long purple robe and his tall rounded hat shone like gold in the light. There was such an unearthly quality about the silent watching figure that the three of them stared for some time.

Then Shrimp shuddered again and grunted. ' It didn't work, you say ! If that isn't a spook I never saw one ! '

Corrigan grinned. ' Did you ever see one ? That's just some wandering tourist.'

Shrimp snorted his disbelief. ' Tourist ? Dressed like that ? '

' Does seem a bit far-fetched,' Corrigan agreed quietly, ' Let's find out ! '

He leapt forward with such speed that Geoff gasped and began to chase after him. As soon as Corrigan moved, the figure out in the desert slipped back into the shadow of the pyramid and disappeared. Corrigan was there in a few seconds, and Shrimp came up after him and they stood and looked around. Geoff came panting up.

' Hey ! ' he gasped. ' Not so fast, you two ! I don't want to be left behind.'

Corrigan smiled. ' What's wrong, Geoff? Don't tell me *you're* scared.'

' I'm not the only one. Shrimp didn't let himself get very far behind.' Geoff was thinking how comfortable it was to be near the powerful bulk of Corrigan at a time like this.

' Shrimp never did,' Corrigan was saying. ' He was about the quickest thing on the rugger field I ever saw.'

' Quick ! ' Shrimp said impatiently. ' What about the chap who was standing here ? He made us all look slow.   Where'd he get to ? '

Corrigan pointed to the shadow along the western side of the pyramid. ' There ! ' he said.

The shadow they were looking into was smothering and velvety. Where they were standing the moonlight was of an unreal brightness : a few feet away lay the black night-shadow cast by the solid stone of the pyramid. ' Into that,' Corrigan went on. ' He'd only have to move a few feet into that shadow and nobody could see him.'

' But you don't understand,' Geoff whispered uncertainly.

' What don't we understand ? ' Corrigan asked.

' About the—the thing we saw. You talk as if it were a man.' Geoff's voice was low and wavering. ' It couldn't have been a man.'

' It wasn't a duck-billed platypus,' Shrimp said gruffly.

' What was it ? ' Corrigan asked.

Geoff cleared his throat. ' Well, I guess I couldn't see the details, I was too far away, but it looked to me like a priest, a Chief Priest of about the time of Tuthmosis. That was how they dressed.'

Shrimp stared at him unbelievingly and Corrigan

gave a low chuckle. ' A Chief Priest of Ancient
Egypt,' he said, ' and he takes size nine in shoes.'
He pointed down to the footprints in the sand.
There were the marks of two shoes, where a man
had stood and shuffled, and the prints were blurred.
' A substantial ghost ! ' Corrigan went on. ' He
must weigh all of twelve stones.'

' But why should a *man* dress like that ? ' Geoff
asked, still in a whisper.

Corrigan shook his head. ' Search me ! It's
all very odd and we're getting cold standing here.
Let's walk and we may find your priest again.'

He led the way along the western side of the
pyramid. It was like stepping out of daylight into
midnight. They walked in silence, Corrigan listening to every sound. He heard the occasional low
sigh from the wind as the great blocks of the
pyramid ruffled it, and the scurrying of a disturbed
lizard, but nothing more. Shrimp was watching.
His eyes ached with staring at the huge black
triangle of Cheops' Pyramid which seemed to be
leaning towards them in the darkness, and, to rest
them, he looked at the moonlit Second Pyramid,
a short distance away. There was no life anywhere.

Geoff had stopped trembling. The watching
silent man, coming right after the spook-talk, scared
me, he said to himself and grinned ruefully.
Talked myself into it, I guess.

They reached the south-western corner of the
Great Pyramid and stepped out into the moonlight
again. Corrigan stopped. ' No sign of our friend,'

he said quietly. ' We have the place to ourselves again. What next, Geoff ? '

Geoff pointed to where they could see the other two big pyramids. ' I'd like to walk along to the far end, to the smallest of the three pyramids,' he answered.

' What do they call it ? ' Shrimp asked.

' That's the Pyramid of Mycerinus. It may be the smallest of the three but it's still pretty massive. The next one, the Second Pyramid, is Chephren's and is nearly as big as the Great Pyramid.'

' So Cheops, Chephren and Mycerinus were buried in these three whacking great things, were they ? ' Corrigan asked.

Geoff nodded. His enthusiasm was coming back. ' They sure were. And the pyramids were built in that order. Hundreds of other people were buried all round them.' He pointed in the direction of the Nile. ' Just over there, in the desert, is where they discovered another pyramid a year or two back. I want to have a look at it. But not now. Right now I'm going to see what sort of a job Mycerinus did for himself. Coming ? '

' Suits me,' Shrimp said.

Corrigan was still thinking about the purple-robed figure. ' You two do that,' he said. ' I've heard that people climb this Great Pyramid and I'd like to have a crack at it. I want to see what the Nile Valley looks like from way up, on a night like this.'

' Okay,' Geoff agreed. ' Go along to the north face. That's the easiest way up. We'll see you

when we get back in about an hour. Let's go,
Shrimp.'

They set off, Shrimp silent and wondering what
Corrigan was up to and Geoff talking pyramids
and tombs with all his old fire.

Corrigan smiled as he watched them go. Then
he turned away and began to walk along the base
of the Great Pyramid. He appeared to be strolling
aimlessly, but in reality he was going quickly and
carefully and his eyes and ears were missing nothing.
About half-way along the southern face he stopped
and looked up to where the pyramid rose like a
stairway to the stars. 'We'll try it here,' he
muttered, and began to climb.

The huge blocks of stone still remembered the
day's heat and were warm. Corrigan was aston-
ished at their size. He had to lift himself vertically
up them and very soon, as he climbed tier after
tier, he was sweating. But he climbed quickly and
steadily, and when he judged himself to be about
half-way up he stopped to look round. He was
looking across the Nile Valley, and to the left the
lights of Cairo glared undimmed up into the sky.
The Sphinx, surprisingly close in the moonlight,
was below him. He made his way quickly along
to the corner of the pyramid, and from there he
could see the other two large pyramids and the
small figures of Geoff and Shrimp just disappearing
round the south-western corner of the second. He
smiled and continued to climb.

A few minutes later he was still climbing and
enjoying the tussle with the stone and the cool

breeze which was now fanning him. He was thinking ; thinking about the thousands who had slaved here and sweated and died to build this world's wonder and leave a mountain of stone for tourists to climb up. Corrigan's little smile showed that he was enjoying himself, and then the smile died and his eyes went cold as he stared across the plateau to where he could see the distant figure of a man who had just stepped out of the blackness beyond the Pyramid of Chephren. The moonlight struck back brightly from his head-dress. It was the man they had seen before, Geoff's priest who took size nine in shoes. Corrigan saw him raise his arm, and a few seconds later he heard the thin echo of a shout and then another, fainter than the first, with only a trace of its anger and despair left in it.

Corrigan turned and began to go down the great stone stairway of the pyramid, leaping lightly from one block to the next and travelling so swiftly that he could feel the rush of the air as it came up to meet him. He was sweating no longer. He was cool and thinking coolly ; thinking about Shrimp and Geoff and blaming himself for having left them. He reached the bottom of the pyramid and began to run with long powerful strides across the sand, making for the south-western corner of the Second Pyramid. In a few minutes he was there, and as he tore round the corner he stumbled against something lying in the moonlight on the sand.

Corrigan recognised it immediately. It was a

He heard the thin echo of a shout

long box, shaped roughly like the human body and painted in faded colours and ancient patterns. It was a coffin of the type used in Old Egypt. Corrigan's heart seemed to pause as he crouched down on the sand and lifted the coffin-lid. Inside, snugly fitting, was the body of a man, a body bound round tightly with strips of white cloth which hid all but the feet. Corrigan touched it gently, and then took out his knife and began feverishly to cut the wrappings from the head. When they fell away he was looking into the dead face of a man he didn't know ; a man who appeared to have been full of good humour in life ; a happy twinkling man who in death was empty and pointless, with a pale and flabby face and a jaunty little dark moustache. It wasn't either Shrimp or Geoff.

Corrigan gave a long sigh and stood up. Inside him a cool and deadly anger was beginning to throb. He started to walk quickly along the side of the pyramid. For a man of his size he walked with astonishing leisurely speed and in menacing silence, driven on by a cold aching urge to get his big hands on the men who had left that coffin for him to find.

He reached the corner of the pyramid and stopped. There was the stealthy sound of breathing. Round that corner, in the black shadow of the pyramid, somebody was waiting. Something like joy surged up in Corrigan and he smiled and glanced up at the pyramid. At this point some of the original limestone remained over the great blocks of stone and it was smoothed by centuries of wind-blown sand. It would be impossible to climb it quietly so Corrigan leapt round the corner swiftly and silently, out of the moonlight into the blackness so suddenly that he felt the coldness of it strike him.

Nobody was there. Corrigan stood still in the darkness and waited for his eyes to focus. He listened. The breathing still went on, and he knew now that it wasn't the breathing of a man crouching in ambush but the rapid jerky breathing of a man having a bad dream. Then Corrigan made out the shape of somebody lying on the sand at the foot of the pyramid. He bent down, and by the clean smell of him and his size he knew it to be Shrimp and he carried him out into the moonlight and laid him on the sand. Shrimp was unconscious and breathing heavily, and there was a swelling bruise on the back of his head and a cut from which the blood had run and was now congealing stickily.

'Shrimp!' Corrigan whispered. 'Shrimp! Wake up, boy!'

Shrimp stirred with a groan, muttered something, and then slipped back into unconsciousness again and Corrigan covered him with his jacket.

He stood up and began to trot along the dark side of the pyramid until he came to the corner. From there he could see the Great Pyramid, propping up the stars, and the Sphinx, but nothing else ; no sign of Geoff. He turned and ran back and, as he went, he heard the distant sound of a car starting, racing up through its gears and droning away into the night.

Shrimp hadn't stirred. Corrigan picked him up gently and easily and began to carry him back, and Shrimp groaned and muttered, ' The Purple Priest.'

' What's that you say, boy ? ' Corrigan asked.

' The Purple Priest. Opi, the Purple Priest,' Shrimp said again, very slowly, his voice trailing off as unconsciousness welled up over him once more.

Corrigan strode quickly across the loose sand, barely noticing the weight of Shrimp's limp body. He was thinking ; thinking about the newly dead man in the old coffin, about the Purple Priest, the Tomb of Opi and about Geoff. He wanted to know the answers to many problems. ' And,' he muttered, thinking aloud, ' I'd particularly like to meet the thugs who've done this. When I get my hands on those boys I'll make 'em squirm.'

He came to the edge of the Pyramid plateau and saw Geoff's deserted Packard below him and the lights of Mena House Hotel in the distance. The car was unlocked and Corrigan gently eased Shrimp on to the rear seat and climbed in behind the wheel. In a few seconds he was whirling away from the desert and back towards Cairo.

Groups of gossiping people were sitting about in front of the Oasis Hotel catching the last of the evening's coolness before going to bed. Corrigan stopped the Packard at the main entrance and lifted Shrimp off the seat and, as he turned, the Sudanese hall-porter came smiling towards him.

' Get Mr Badri,' Corrigan said, ' and get him

quickly. Ask him to come to Mr Bradley's room right away.'

He carried Shrimp, all dangling helplessness, through the foyer, where he neither saw the stares of the lounging guests nor heard the stir of their excitement, and into the lift. In a few seconds he had Shrimp on his bed and was beginning to undress him. He worked quickly and silently, and he knew when Badri's crêpe-soled feet brought him cat-like across the thick carpet of the room.

' I want you, Mr Badri,' he said, and he heard the little gasp from behind him.

Badri started again when Corrigan turned round. Here was somebody he had never seen before ; the same body, the same great breadth of shoulder and depth of chest ; but the face ! The square chin, the hard mouth, the cold boring eyes were those of a Mr Corrigan he had not yet met. He trembled.

' What is it that I do for you, Mr Corrigan ? ' he asked. ' Your friend is ill, perhaps ? ' His voice was growing silky again. ' Is the heat tonight. Or is perhaps that he drinks too much ? '

' I'll tell you what's wrong with my friend,' Corrigan answered in a level tone, ' and save you the trouble of having any more nasty guesses, because they annoy me, Mr Badri, and if I get annoyed I might do something which you would regret afterwards. My friend has concussion. He's been hit over the head by some lousy Egyptian thugs. If you know any lousy Egyptian thugs, Mr Badri, tell them I'm looking for the ones who did this, and when I find them I'm going to get very cross with them.' He smiled, a great beaming smile of icy charm, and Badri trembled again. ' Now would you mind getting a doctor ? ' Corrigan went on. ' I'd like him to be here as soon as possible.'

Badri bowed. 'I go, Mr Corrigan. I telephone.'

' And while you're at it, get the police.'

The Egyptian had reached the door of the room. He stopped, fingering his bottom lip, and turned. ' The police, Mr Corrigan ? '

Corrigan was covering Shrimp with the bed-clothes. ' The police,' he repeated. ' You do have police in Egypt, I suppose ? '

' But of course.'

' Well, get them. And make it somebody important. Mr Bradley, who is a British subject, has been clouted over the head with what is known as a blunt instrument, and Mr Oppenheimer, an American citizen, has disappeared. Whitehall and Washington are going to say some undiplomatic things to Cairo if we don't have action quickly.'

Badri was walking back slowly into the room. His face was in shadow and his eyes shone with all the cunning of the ages. ' Not only is it that Mr Bradley is wounded,' he said, ' but also that Mr Oppenheimer has disappeared. Could it not be that Mr Oppenheimer attacks Mr Bradley and runs away ? Is possible ? '

Corrigan stood up slowly and towered over the Egyptian, his fair head bending over the black one. ' Mr Badri,' he said softly, ' you're tempting me.'

Badri smiled. ' You think this is possible ? '

Corrigan shook his head. ' No, it isn't that that tempts me.'

' But what is it, Mr Corrigan ? '

' You're tempting me to lose my temper. So far I'm resisting the temptation, but don't push me.' Corrigan smiled and leaned forward. ' Now will you go and get that doctor and the police ? ' he whispered.

Ahmed Badri hurried out of the room and, as he went, Shrimp stirred in the bed and groaned. ' The Tomb of Opi ! ' he said in a loud voice. ' Tomb of Opi ! '

Corrigan bent over him. ' Relax, boy. You're okay. As soon as you're fit again we'll find this tomb and take it apart.'

He missed the look in Badri's eyes, the glitter of excitement which showed for a few seconds as the Egyptian walked through the door.

Chapter III

HASHEESH

Shrimp was in bed trying to put things in order. He knew that he was in his room and that the morning sun was laying broad patches of light on the carpet. The window was open and the mosquito-curtain was fluttering in the little breeze. He knew that his bandaged head was aching with a steady vindictive throb, and that this surged up into waves of pain which broke against his brittle skull every time he moved.

He tried to concentrate. He remembered visiting the moonlit pyramids with Corrigan and Geoff; he remembered walking with Geoff and he recalled the great shadow behind the Second Pyramid. He knew he had plunged into that shadow. . . .

The door opened and Corrigan came into the room, followed by a tall uniformed Egyptian. Corrigan, grinning, stood and looked down at Shrimp. ' So you've decided to wake up ! You've had a long sleep, son ; something like fourteen hours solid. How d'you feel ? '

Shrimp's dry throat cracked when he tried to answer. ' Vague, floaty,' he whispered. ' What's happened ? How did I get here ? '

' I brought you back and put you to bed. The doctor came last night and again this morning. You have concussion and you're to stay in bed for the rest of the day. After that you ought to be okay.'

' I was knocked out, wasn't I ? '

' I'll say ! We'll go into that later. Luckily you're blessed with a hard head.' Corrigan turned to the Egyptian. ' First I want to introduce you to Colonel Mustafa Hadrashi of the Egyptian Police. He was here last night and I told him the story as I knew it. Now he wants your version. Do you feel up to it ? '

Shrimp nodded and winced. Colonel Hadrashi was a tall spare man with a thin bony face. He had an eagle-beak nose and two small bright eyes which looked as hard as diamonds. His hair was cropped short. Shrimp reflected that the outlook for the criminals of Cairo must be poor.

The Colonel sat down. ' Can you tell me, Mr Bradley, who attacks you ? ' he asked.

Shrimp cleared his throat, started to speak and then stopped. He was remembering more of last night. ' Where's Geoff ? ' he asked suddenly.

There was a moment's silence and then Corrigan sat on the edge of the bed. ' We don't know, Shrimp,' he answered. ' I found you unconscious, but there was no sign of Geoff. He's gone and we haven't found him yet. That's why Colonel Hadrashi's here.'

Shrimp let it sink in. More trouble, he thought. We seem to collect it. Poor old Geoff ! ' We must find him,' he said in a stronger voice. ' The Priest has him. They'll put him in a coffin, like the other chap.'

Corrigan and the Colonel sat and watched him.
After a few moments Corrigan spoke.

' Sort it out, Shrimp. Tell us from the beginning
in your own words.'

' We were walking past the pyramid,' Shrimp
began, ' the second one, the Pyramid of Cheph—
something.'

' Chephren,' Hadrashi said quietly.

' We'd taken a long time getting there because
Geoff was telling me all the Egyptology in the
world. He showed me the other tombs, the flat
ones, and explained how they'd gradually been
developed into pyramids. Great stuff, this Egyptology ! Then we hurried and Geoff said we ought
to go round the Third Pyramid from the other
side.' Shrimp started to sweat, the dampness
breaking suddenly out of his skin.

' Take it easy, boy,' Corrigan said quietly.
' There's no hurry. Try some of this lime-water.'

Shrimp felt the bitter sweetness of the liquid
soaking into his parched tongue. He sighed. ' We
were almost at the corner of the pyramid—
Chephren's—when a man stepped from the shadow
out into the moonlight about fifty yards ahead.
He stood looking at us and we stopped. It was the
Priest.' Shrimp smiled. ' It stops there.'

Colonel Hadrashi nodded. ' Your story stops
there, Mr Bradley ? '

' I think so,' Shrimp answered uncertainly.

' You mean,' the Colonel went on, ' that you
are not sure how much of this happened and how
much you dream, is it not ? '

'That's true,' Shrimp agreed. 'I probably dreamt the whole thing after I was knocked out.' He shook his head doubtfully. 'I may not even have been knocked out. I could have had a fall, I suppose.'

'You didn't dream any of it,' Corrigan said. 'It all happened, Shrimp. I saw that so-called Priest step out into the moonlight and very soon after that I heard you shout. I was half-way up the Great Pyramid at the time.' He grinned suddenly. 'I never did reach the top. I must do it some time.'

Shrimp's eyes were clearing. It was coming right now, like getting the knots out of tangled wool. 'Then the rest of it must have happened,' he said. 'Geoff and I stopped. I said I was going to have a closer look at this priestly joker and we moved forward. As soon as we were past the corner of the pyramid we were rushed by four men. They were waiting for us.'

'Describe them, please,' Hadrashi interrupted.

'They were dressed like anybody else—in ordinary lounge suits. But they were wearing masks. There was nothing priestly about them. They were pretty tough boys and we had an unholy scrap. That's why I shouted, Corrigan, when I realised we couldn't make it against the four of them.'

Corrigan nodded. 'Sure. What happened?'

Shrimp smiled suddenly. 'Geoff fights like an overgrown spider, all long arms and legs and no technique. But he managed to get a few useful cracks in before one of the men came up behind

him and socked him with a blackjack. He went
down cold. It didn't last long after that. There
were four of them, Corrigan, and they took a bit of
holding,' he ended apologetically.

' I'll bet they knew they'd been in a fight.' Corrigan grinned. ' Pity I wasn't there to lend a hand.'

Shrimp nodded. ' If you'd been with us we'd
have massacred them. I'd like to have another go
when the odds aren't so heavy.'

' You shall,' Corrigan said quietly, ' and next
time I'll be with you. We'll soften 'em, boy. What
happened next ? '

' They dragged me to my feet and two of them
held me. Then they brought one of those Ancient
Egyptian coffins out of the shadow and put it down
in front of me. I was still a bit foggy after the
scrap. But there was a body in that coffin—a man,
I think—wrapped up like a mummy. Then the
Priest came gliding up.'

' The Priest,' Hadrashi repeated. ' What is
this Priest like ? '

' Nothing on earth,' Shrimp answered with a
shiver. ' Like something you dream about after
too much supper. He was dressed in a long purple
robe with a big golden disc on the front of it—on
the breast. On his head was a sort of tall helmet
of smooth polished gold. It was about a foot high
and it curved up to a blunt point. He was masked
and the mask is gold too, or it looked like it. It
was beaten to the shape of his face, like a death-
mask. I could see his eyes in the slits.' He
shivered again.

'Pleasant character,' Corrigan murmured. 'Do you know him, Colonel?'

Hadrashi shook his head thoughtfully. 'I have not heard of this one before. Did he speak, Mr Bradley?'

Shrimp nodded. 'Yes. He pointed to the body in the coffin and spoke in a voice which sounded hollow—empty. I think he was disguising it. He said, " This happens to all who seek my eternal habitation. I am Opi, Chief Priest of Amun-Ré and Grand Vizier of the North and South. I go before One into the Temple ".'

' " One " ? ' Corrigan queried.

'I think I understand this,' the Colonel said. 'This is a way they have in Ancient Egypt when they speak of the Pharaoh. They call him " One ". Did he say more, please?'

'Yes. He pointed to Geoff and went on : " This American would violate my tomb. Him I take. He would see my tomb : he *shall* see it. You, Englishman, you go to England and do not wait, and take the other, the large Englishman, with you ".'

Corrigan grinned. 'That 'll be me!'

Shrimp moved in the bed. 'And Geoff? You haven't found him yet?'

'Not yet,' Corrigan answered. 'The Colonel's on the job. I told you he had my side of the story last night, but I couldn't tell him very much. Anyway he has men working on it now, and you and I'll be joining the hunt just as soon as you're fit.'

' And what about our plane to England ? '

' We've got three days yet, my lad, and if we miss it there'll be another.'

Shrimp looked uneasy. ' We always seem to run into trouble, Corrigan. We're supposed to be on leave.'

Corrigan nodded. ' Sure. Do you want another crack at those thugs or don't you ? Do you want to go home and leave Geoff or do you want to lend a hand ? '

Shrimp could feel those uncomfortable pale-blue eyes looking into his mind. He struggled with himself for a moment and then he smiled suddenly. ' I certainly do ! I'm not leaving Egypt until we've found Geoff and until I've laid hands on the sweep who knocked me out. That's what happened, you know. As soon as the Priest had finished talking, somebody must have come up behind me and put me to sleep with a blackjack. I don't remember it. I remember nothing more until I woke up this morning.'

Corrigan was nodding and smiling, a hard determined little smile. ' Right ! ' he said quietly. ' We'll do it, boy. We'll go after this Opi, even if he is three thousand and five hundred years old. Looks like you've found yourself some help, Colonel. Do you mind a couple of amateurs butting in ? '

A weary smile wrinkled the brown skin of Hadrashi's worried face. ' I accept your help, Mr Corrigan. Already my men have too much work. But I insist that you take no risks.'

' We never do,' Shrimp murmured from the

(1,824)   4

bed, and his eyes, as he looked at Corrigan, were
beginning to sparkle with puckish excitement.

'How much can you tell us, Colonel, before we
start?' Corrigan asked.

'About what, please?'

'About the Tomb of Opi and this Priest.'

Hadrashi shook his head doubtfully. 'Nothing.
Never have we heard of this Priest. Is something
more.' He scratched his hooked nose thoughtfully.
'Always new criminals arise and always we have
no more men to fight them.'

'You think the Priest is just another criminal
then?' Corrigan asked.

'I know not.' The Colonel shrugged. 'Maleesh!
It is no matter. It is what he does that is criminal.'

'What does he do?'

'He attacks Mr Bradley and he kidnaps Mr
Oppenheimer. Is it not enough? In one night he
does this to the citizens of two powerful nations.'

'He also killed a man, the man in the coffin,'
Corrigan reminded him.

Shrimp was keeping quiet. He felt tired, and
he knew that Corrigan would squeeze the Colonel
dry of information by his steady suggestive questions.

Hadrashi stroked his nose again. 'Yes. Is
that also. He murders, does this Priest. If Allah
wills, we catch him.' He sighed.

Corrigan waited, watching the Egyptian. He
could see the worry and strain in the deep-set eyes
and the puffiness around them : sleep-hunger was
showing in the dark face. 'Tell us, Colonel,' he
said. 'Tell us about the dead man.'

Hadrashi rasped his rough hand across his face.
' I tell you. I do not explain. This I cannot do.
You know that in England you have your MI5 ? '

Corrigan nodded. ' Sure. Secret Service.'

'That is correct. This man you find last night,
I know him. He is in what is our MI5, our Security
Service. He is Greek, but he lives in Egypt and his
parents also and their parents also. So he is Greek
but he is Egyptian. You understand this ? '

' Yes,' Corrigan answered. ' But what has he
to do with the Tomb of Opi ? '

Hadrashi shrugged. ' This I do not know.
But I tell you something.' He leaned forward.
' This Greek is in our Security Service. He works
in the clothes of a civilian ; I in uniform. Understand ? But we work, the two of us, on the same
job. And this has nothing to do with the Tomb of
Opi. We are not Egyptologists. We leave that to
the Department of Antiquities.'

Corrigan was nodding thoughtfully. ' So it
appears that the Purple Priest has nothing to do
with you, yet he kills one of your colleagues. The
first thing is to find his tomb. Don't you agree,
Mr Badri ? '

Shrimp's eyes sprang open and the Colonel
jerked round. Standing behind them was Ahmed
Badri. He looked languid and lazy ; only in his
eyes did life glint. His smile—deferential, friendly,
helpful, perhaps mocking—was always there.

' You come into a room very quietly, Mr Badri,
but not quietly enough,' Corrigan was saying. ' I
didn't hear you knock.'

'But yes, Mr Corrigan, I do knock.   But I do all so quietly because Mr Bradley he is ill.   Is it not?'

'It is not,' Shrimp grunted.   'I'm fine!'

Corrigan was watching Badri.   'And what do you want?' he asked.

'I come to ask if there is something you need. Is hot here and you talk.   Coffee, perhaps?'

Corrigan shook his head.   'Thank you, no. Mr Bradley mustn't have coffee today.'

Badri bowed slightly.   'Yes, Mr Corrigan.   I go.   If it is that you need something I will be here.'

He turned towards the door.   He was dressed in a suit of light worsted and on his head was the usual red tarboosh.   Corrigan had never seen him without it.   Wonder if he sleeps in it, he said to himself.

'There is one thing,' he said aloud.   'Mr Bradley and I are going to have a look for this Tomb of Opi.   You remember Mr Oppenheimer was intending to look for it?   Have you any idea where we might begin?'

Badri stopped and paused for a few moments before turning to face them, and his eyes, when they saw them, were as deeply mysterious as ever, while his full lips were just beginning to make themselves smile.   Corrigan wished that he had asked the question earlier, while he was watching the Egyptian's face.

Badri shrugged.   'Is impossible that anybody helps you with this, Mr Corrigan.   Nobody knows.

The tomb is in Jebel Ataka and the Jebel is so big.'

' I thought you might know more than we do. After all, you're an Egyptologist, while we know nothing.'

Badri was smiling now. ' Is the same for everybody. Everybody knows nothing about the Tomb of Opi. I shall be happy if you have good luck.' He bowed and left them.

Colonel Hadrashi was studying Corrigan's little smile. It was of the mouth and not of the eyes and it chilled.

' You have good hearing, Mr Corrigan,' he said. ' I did not hear Ahmed Badri enter the room.'

Corrigan nodded and smiled. ' I happened to be listening, that's all. My ears are no better than yours.'

' They relieve the monotony of his face,' Shrimp said slyly.

Hadrashi looked puzzled. ' Yes ? ' he said doubtfully.

' My friend is trying to be funny,' Corrigan explained with a grin. ' He often tries but rarely succeeds.' He became thoughtful. ' I'm still wondering why Badri came here. Tell me, Colonel, is he okay ? Do you know anything against him ? '

Hadrashi shrugged. ' I know things against many men, Mr Corrigan. But about Mr Badri I know nothing which can concern the attack on your friend. He manages this hotel, and he has made himself known because of his interest in the

past. He is—how is it?—eccentric? Is no crime
to be eccentric. He thinks that he is descended
from one of the great ones of Ancient Egypt.'

'From Opi, in fact?'

Hadrashi nodded. 'Is so. Is strange that, but
not criminal. Is there any other way in which I
help before I leave?'

Corrigan thought for a moment before replying.
'There are two things I'd like to know. First, can
you suggest any way in which we can get an idea
where this Tomb of Opi may be?'

The Colonel sat thinking and tapping his knee.
At last he looked up. 'Is one man who may help.
This man, he knows many things about Egypt today
and in the past. His name is Pappadikos. Is many
things, this Pappadikos. He sells the cotton of
Egypt; trades in animals for zoos; sells curios
and antiques and other things.' He smiled. 'Is
many things and knows many people. You see
him. He has a shop in Soliman Pasha Street. Go
along the street on its left, and almost at Midan
Soliman Pasha you find a little shop where curios
and antiques are sold. There you find Pappadikos.
Is possible that he helps. He knows many people.
There is nobody else.' He shrugged. 'I do not
think this tomb is important.'

Corrigan smiled. 'No? Well, I'm going to
try it. Odd name—Pappadikos. Greek?'

'Yes. Everybody in Egypt knows Pappa
Pappadikos. He was Greek but he is Egyptian.'
Hadrashi's troubled thoughts showed in his dark-
ening face. 'I tell you. Pappadikos and the

man you find in the coffin last night they were
brothers.'   .

Corrigan sat up. ' That's a bit of a coincidence !
Does he know his brother's been murdered ? '

' He knows. He will talk to you. What else is
it that you would know ? '

' I probably have a nerve to ask this. You told
us that the dead man was working with you—you're
on the same job. This man is connected with the
disappearance of Geoff Oppenheimer because he
must have been murdered by the gang of kid-
nappers. Can you tell me what you're working
on ? '

Shrimp wriggled up in the bed. ' There's
another connection, Corrigan, one we've just heard
about. The murdered man is the brother of the
chap we have to get in touch with about the tomb.
Which is another coincidence.'

' That's a point,' Corrigan said softly. ' There
are so many coincidences in this business that I'm
getting dizzy.' He was watching the Egyptian's
face and he thought he knew the reason for
Hadrashi's frown of concentration. He doesn't
know how much to tell us, he said to himself. He
wants us to help, but he's scared of telling things
we aren't supposed to know.

The Colonel sat nodding like a mechanical toy
for a long time while they waited. Then he sat
up. ' It is so,' he said in a firm voice. ' I tell you.
This Pappadikos, the seller of curios, is, as I have
said, brother to Pappadikos of the Security Service.
That is coincidence. Yes ? Pappa Pappadikos

knows all people and is known by all. He has
friends who are princes and friends who are criminals. All know his brother is in the Security
Service.'

' You mean,' Corrigan interrupted, ' that people
—even criminals—tell him their secrets in spite of
the fact that his brother is in your Security Service.
They must trust him.'

' Is correct, that. Is what I mean. His brother
and I work, not together, but on the same work.
Understand ? I should not, but I will tell you
about this work.' He leaned forward. ' You know
hasheesh ? '

' The drug ? ' Corrigan said.

' Made from hemp,' Shrimp volunteered.

Hadrashi nodded. ' Is right. For long time
now *hasheesh* is smuggled into Egypt. Hemp is
grown in several of the countries of the Mediter-
ranean. It is illegal to grow it but it is sown with
other crops so that it is not seen, and harvested and
smuggled into my country.' He swallowed, and
his eyes, like burnished jet, were liquid with emotion.
' I fail to catch these smugglers. Now——'

Corrigan was holding up his hand. ' A minute,
Colonel. I thought I heard something.'

He rose quietly and, even as he moved, they
heard the sound of footsteps padding stealthily away
from the door. Corrigan leapt forward, wrenched
open the door and stood in the passage outside,
shaking his head.

He came back into the room. ' Somebody's
interested in our conversation. I'd give something

to know who it was. We must keep our voices low.' He sat on the bed. 'You were telling us about *hasheesh*, Colonel.'

'Yes. I continue.' Hadrashi looked troubled. 'Is everywhere the same. Spies! Spies! Spies!' He threw up his hands. 'I tell you about *hasheesh*. It comes to Egypt but is not all used here. No. It is collected by an organisation—gang, yes?— and is smuggled out again. It goes to India, Africa, America; England too. This is going on now for three, four years and it does much harm. I try to catch this gang, and what have I done?' He snapped his fingers. 'Not so much!' He wagged his head from side to side. 'Oh, a truck at the frontier with a bag of hemp now and then; sometimes a man smoking it; but that is all. We do not know the gang, who leads it or where its headquarters are, and the few we catch they do not know these things either. That is our work.'

Corrigan nodded thoughtfully. 'And where does the Purple Priest come into all this?'

Hadrashi's lips curled. 'Pah! Him? He does not!'

'Then why did he murder your colleague Pappadikos?'

For a moment the Colonel was nonplussed. 'That is something else I do not know. Another coincidence?' He smiled and shook his head. 'Ah, the things about this that I do not know! Many, too many.' His voice dropped to a whisper. 'We think that this gang works from Suez, not from Cairo. In Suez are many ships. We *think* this : we do not know it.' He stood up suddenly. 'And now I go. I hope that Mr Bradley is soon well.'

Corrigan slid off the bed. ' Yes. Thanks for taking us into your confidence, Colonel. We'll respect it.'

' If I think you will not, I do not tell you these things. It is not only the Sphinx that can keep his mouth closed.'

Corrigan smiled. ' Thanks again. If we get on to anything we'll let you know.'

' Yes. Do nothing unless you inform me. Is dangerous, this Egypt of ours.' The Colonel walked towards the door.

Corrigan, about to open it, paused and held out his hand. ' With all your troubles you won't forget Geoff Oppenheimer, will you, Colonel ? '

Hadrashi shook hands. ' I promise you Mr Oppenheimer is priority until we find him—dead or alive. I hope alive.'

' Me too,' Shrimp said quietly from the bed.

Chapter IV

'RAMESES, HE TELLS'

Corrigan walked steadily along the seething street
named after Soliman Pasha. It is a wide street
and a smelly street, where the mixture of spicy
Eastern smells and Western petrol fumes hangs
heavily over the hot dust and where people are
always hurrying and talking loudly.

The people jostling around Corrigan were
mainly Egyptians and mostly men in lounge suits,
cheap thin suits in un-Western colours. Everywhere tasselled tarbooshes bobbed on dark heads,
and above them Corrigan's fair head shone as he
moved through the crowd which slipped past on
each side of him.

He was smiling slightly at two men who were
walking hand-in-hand ahead of him, when a shop
sign caught his eye and he stopped. It was a small
shop, with a dusty window which displayed a
jumble of funerary statuettes, papyrus rolls and
modern imitation scarab brooches. Above the door
was the name 'Pappadikos', and a card pinned
aslant in the window was printed in pencil with
the words 'English speaking'.

Corrigan opened the door and started the mad
jangling of a tin bell. He walked inside. The
shop was tiny and was cluttered up with ancient
and undusted junk, while the air held the dead

sweetness of a tomb. Through a screen of glass
beads a man came from the back of the shop.
Corrigan looked at him, wondering what sort of
man he had expected to see. What he saw was a
round little man with a fat shining face, greying
hair and a huge moustache as wide as his ears and
twisted into a waxen point at each end.

'Mr Pappadikos?' Corrigan inquired.

The Greek spread his hands. 'You are Engleesh,'
he said, and his voice had a lilt in it. 'You do
not come to buy. The Engleesh never come to
buy from Pappa. American, yes; Engleesh, no.
They come to ask for something.' He wiped his face
wearily. 'What is it you want, big Engleeshman?'

Corrigan grinned. 'If it'll make you feel any
better I'll buy something.'

'Yes? You buy what?'

Corrigan was still smiling. 'You haven't any
Ancient Egyptian coffins for sale? They're just
the thing for hiding the bodies of your Security
Service men.'

The Greek's eyes flashed and Corrigan noticed
them for the first time. They were blue and almost
buried in the deep flesh of his face and they seemed
to be dancing with amusement. 'This I do not
understand,' Pappadikos was saying. 'These men
—these Security Service men—they live lives of
danger, and lives of danger end—pouff! Like
that! It is no matter when you die, Engleeshman.
What matters is *how* you die and *why* you die.
Now! I think we talk too much and I think you
joke with Pappa. No?'

' Yes,' Corrigan said.

' I know it. You do not come to buy. I am poor, I starve, and Engleeshmen come to ask me questions.' He threw up his hands. ' What is it you want ? '

' Colonel Hadrashi sent me.' Corrigan's eyes never left the Greek's face. He was trying to get past the shining flesh and the dancing eyes to find out what was going on in a brain which he guessed to be quick and shrewd. ' He said you might be able to help me.'

Pappadikos was stroking his chin. ' Colonel Hadrashi ? ' he murmured. ' Somewhere I hear of this Colonel. Do I know him ? '

' He knows you. Probably he knew your brother better.'

Again the eyes danced and Corrigan realised that it was anger that was making them so lively. ' I think my brother will be left out of this, Engleeshman. This is the day of his funeral. You know this ? '

Corrigan nodded. ' I know he's dead—murdered—and I'm sorry. I found him.'

Pappadikos blew out his cheeks and let the air explode from his mouth. ' Boh ! You must be the Engleeshman, Corrigan. Now I know it. You come to bring your sympathy. That is good, ver' good. I thank you for myself, my brother's wife and children and the souls of my father and mother. Pappa Pappadikos thanks you, Mr Corrigan. Now goodbye ! '

Corrigan smiled. ' I'm not going anywhere. I haven't told you why I came.'

The Greek's bushy eyebrows went up. ' No ? You want something ? I know it ! Always you Engleesh want something, but not to buy. What is it, please ? '

' Where is the Tomb of Opi ? '

Pappadikos blinked, but failed to hide his flicker of surprise. ' Again please ? ' he said. He looked at the sun-tanned face above him and saw the square jaw, the straight line of the mouth, the eyes which told him nothing and the expression which suggested humour, tolerance and something else ; something difficult to pin down : the gift which some men have for commanding respect and obedience. He nodded thoughtfully.

' I asked where is the Tomb of Opi ? ' Corrigan was saying.

Pappa shrugged. ' I do not sell *tombs*. I sell curios and antiques ; I deal in cotton and rare animals ; but I do not sell tombs. How am I knowing where this Tomb of Opi is ? '

Corrigan was smiling a discomfiting little smile. ' Colonel Hadrashi said you might help. Apparently you don't want to.'

' Why you want this tomb ? You are an Egyptologist ? '

' No, I'm a rubber-planter.'

' Again, please ? '

' I'm a rubber-planter. I grow rubber.'

Pappadikos shook his head in bewilderment. ' You grow rubber ? Here we use it for auto tyres. You plant rubber in this tomb ? '

' No. I'm looking for Geoff Oppenheimer.'

The Greek blew out his cheeks. ' Geoff Oppenheimer ? Is this a man ? Is it *his* tomb ? '

' He isn't dead, I hope.'

Pappa threw up his hands and his sigh was full
of resignation. ' What is this ? You grow rubber
in the tomb of a man who is not dead ? You—
how is it ?—you pull my legs, my big friend ?
Yes ? '

Corrigan's eyes were cold and unfriendly. ' No,
I don't pull your legs. I'm particular about the
legs I pull. I come here for help and I get nothing.
I've an idea you aren't interested in helping.'

The bead-screen tinkled and another man
came from the room at the back of the shop.
He was wearing dark sun-glasses. It was Ahmed
Badri.

' Mr Corrigan is the persistent tomb-seeker,' he
murmured. ' It is not always wise to seek tombs
in Egypt today, Mr Corrigan.'

Corrigan smiled. ' No ? And why not ? '

' Is sometimes dangerous. A man may find a
tomb he does not seek.'

' You don't say ! Tell me, Mr Badri,' Corrigan
said, moving forward softly, ' how do you manage
always to pop up when I don't want you ? '

Badri saw something in Corrigan's eyes. He
didn't like it. He stepped back. ' But, Mr Corrigan, it is coincidence ! That is it—coincidence ! '

' Really ? There are more coincidences than
flies in this country.' Corrigan smiled. ' If it
happens again, my dear Badri, I might begin to
get suspicious.'

Badri overdid the expression of pain which came into his eyes. 'But, Mr Corrigan, I come to see my friend ! I am interested in the things of Ancient Egypt which he collects.'

Corrigan looked over the pair of them, the fat little Greek and the plump smiling Egyptian. 'Okay,' he said. 'You came to see your friend. I'll leave you to it.'

Pappadikos had been silent for too long. Now he flapped his hand on the top of the counter.

'You go now ? You buy nothing from Pappa ? Always it is the same with you Engleesh. You come, you ask questions, you make the joke and you buy nothing ! ' He took a little roll of papyrus from beneath the counter. 'I sell you this. Genuine Middle Kingdom papyrus. I sell for one hundred *piastres*. You buy ? Yes ? '

'No,' Corrigan said quietly.

'Fifty *piastres* ! '

'No. I don't want any papyrus. I think you may have what I do want but you aren't ready to part with it, yet. I'll see you again.' Corrigan smiled at them, and turned and walked out of the shop along which the long shadows of the late afternoon were pointing.

He walked swiftly and, as he went, his brain worked quickly, his thoughts going in circles. I'm getting nowhere, he said to himself. Everywhere it's the same—the smiling Eastern politeness, the soft answers, the smooth talk and the mocking eyes. Everywhere I'm up against a barrier of Eastern mystery. They've put up a sign : ' No Westerners allowed inside '—but I want to get inside. I *must* get inside if I'm ever going to find Geoff.

He came to Opera Square and Ezbekiah Gardens and beyond them to the Old City; the Old City with its narrow streets, its native thousands, its smells and noises, and its mud-brick single-storey buildings with their unfinished walls which stopped above the ground floor, as if the builders had tired of their work.

Corrigan kept walking, but now his eyes were missing nothing. He saw the swarming Egyptians, many of them here in flowing Arab clothes, who stared at him with curiosity, with enmity or with indifference. He went past the end of a dirty little alley and stopped. Somebody had whispered. Out of all the babel of the street his ears had picked a sound intended for him. He turned. A man was leaning against the white-washed mud wall at the corner of the alley, an untidy Egyptian in tarboosh, cheap Western suit and pointed patent-leather shoes. About him was an unbrushed look and from him came an unwashed smell.

' Say that again,' Corrigan said.

The Egyptian smirked and took the cigarette out of the corner of his mouth. ' Tomb of Opi,' he repeated in a quiet voice.

Corrigan walked up to him. ' What do you know about it ? ' he asked.

' Nothing, *Effendi*. I take you to man who tells you. You follow, *Effendi* ? Yes ? '

Corrigan smiled. This is such an obvious trap, he thought, that it stinks. In fact most things

around here seem to stink. If I were subtle and
crafty I wouldn't go within a mile of that alley.
He nodded to the Egyptian. ' Okay. Lead the
way. I'll be right behind you.'

The triumph in the Egyptian's eyes was so
undisguised that Corrigan almost laughed. The
possibility of action had started his blood racing.
He felt strong and confident. If the Egyptian had
not been in such a hurry he would have seen the
cool glint in Corrigan's eyes and he might have
wondered. Instead he turned down the deserted
alley which was so narrow that it squeezed out
most of the afternoon light, and Corrigan followed
him. As he turned the corner Corrigan noticed
that the people in the street he was leaving were
watching in silence and with frank expectancy.
He was walking noiselessly through the dust and
dirt, watching the back of the Egyptian in front of
him, watching the dark doorways and the shadows,
and listening. He was listening for one sound,
staking everything on hearing it. When they had
gone about twenty yards he heard it, a little tell-
tale rustle behind him.

Something like joy surged up in Corrigan and
he laughed, and the laugh was so cold and deadly
that the Egyptian in front of him stopped and
shuddered as Corrigan's hand dropped on his neck
like a vice. Then Corrigan whirled to meet a
second Egyptian who was rushing him from behind
and who already had a knife lifted for the plunge.
Things happened with a speed that devastated the
Egyptians. The first was picked up by his neck

and hurled into the garbage on the ground ; the second found his wrist gripped by fingers which squeezed until the little bones began to crunch. He strained. He wriggled and the sweat started from the skin of his face, and all he could see was the pair of mercilessly cold blue eyes above him. He moaned and dropped the knife.

The other Egyptian had risen shakily to his feet and his eyes were shifting about quickly as he looked for some way out. He would have climbed the walls to escape from this terrible huge Englishman with the awful joy in his eyes, but he was too late. The Englishman had him again, had him by the neck and he was dying, dying slowly.

'*Effendi !* ' he croaked. '*Effendi !* Mercy, and Allah will bless you.'

Then the second Egyptian, the one with the crushed wrist, wriggled and his slimy skin slipped out of Corrigan's fingers. He darted across the narrow street into the blackness of an open doorway.

Corrigan let him go. ' I still have *you*, stinker,' he said, ' and you're going to talk. So start now.' He pulled the Egyptian towards him and shook him. ' There are one or two things I want to know. First, where's the Tomb of Opi ? '

The jibbering Egyptian's eyes rolled and showed their unhealthy whites. ' I talk, *Effendi*, I tell,' he gasped.

Then a foreign sound, a little alien metallic noise, made Corrigan spin round, and he spun the Egyptian with him. He saw in the doorway opposite a spurt of flame, a little finger of fire which pointed at him and he ducked.

The Egyptian was saying 'Tomb of Opi, *Effendi*', when he stopped. Something had hit him in the chest and he coughed, he looked surprised and his legs wavered. ' The Tomb, *Effendi*,' he whispered. ' Rameses, he tells.' He coughed again. ' Allah ! Allah ! ' he murmured ; the life left him and he slumped.

Corrigan lowered him gently to the ground. ' Rameses ? ' he repeated. ' Rameses ? ' He stood up. He knew that the bullet which had killed the Egyptian had been meant for him. ' Time I wasn't here,' he muttered, and ran quickly back down the alley.

When he reached the street he saw immediately that it was deserted. People were skulking in doorways and peeping out of shadows. He began to walk back towards Opera Square. Before he had gone fifty yards he saw a silent group of men coming to meet him. They were all young and were dressed in cheap Western clothes and a red fez. There were about twenty of them and they were spanning the street purposefully. Corrigan knew that they were coming for him. He glanced about. Ahead of him and across the street was an empty doorway and he darted for it. The Egyptians shouted and ran towards him.

Corrigan's back was against the door. He smiled. Something in the smile, in the set of his big body, something in the look of him stopped the mob and they hesitated in front of him, shouting and gesticulating, trying to whip up their mob-courage. A tall bony man whose Adam's Apple bobbed as he shouted seemed to be the leader and Corrigan watched him carefully. Suddenly there was a rush from the left and three snarling men came in, their eyes murderous. It was difficult to follow what happened when they reached Corrigan in the doorway. The middle Egyptian ran on to Corrigan's fist. It lifted him and hurled him backwards and he fell, his mouth broken and bleeding, into the mob. The two remaining Egyptians appeared to be picked up, dashed together and dropped in a heap on the ground, and there was Corrigan, calm, and smiling at the rest of them.

'Come on, boys,' he said. 'No favouritism. Everybody gets the same treatment.'

The Egyptians growled and chattered amongst themselves. The lanky leader was screaming frenziedly and tongue-lashing his men to make them try again, but the next attack never started. Instead down the street came a little convoy of cars, a siren wailing and dust rolling up, and the mob scattered. Before they could get away Corrigan was among them. He grabbed the leader and held him, kicking and helpless.

'I want you, Charlie.' He grinned.

The convoy stopped in a smother of dust, and Corrigan saw that behind the leading car were three vans and out of them determined policemen were tumbling and beginning to collect stragglers from the mob. Out of the car stepped Colonel

Hadrashi, his beak-of-a-nose jutting and his black
eyes flashing.

'Mr Corrigan!' he called. 'You are safe?'

'Never felt better!' Corrigan shook the
rattling bony Egyptian. 'I've a present for you,
Colonel. The local team's cheer-leader! He
doesn't fight, he promotes.'

He sent the Egyptian staggering into the arms
of a waiting policeman who took him away to one
of the vans. Corrigan watched him go and then
turned back to Hadrashi.

'Nice to see you, Colonel.' He smiled. 'How
did you manage to turn up just at the right time?
Another of these Egyptian coincidences?'

The Colonel shook his head. 'Not a coincidence, Mr Corrigan. Is planned with care, all this.
I have you followed. My man is with you all the
afternoon, but he loses you in Ezbekiah Gardens.
Is bad that he loses you. But he informs me, when
he does not find you, that you go to the Old City.
So I come.'

'Good thing too. I don't mind a bit of a
rough-house when it's forced on me, but this was a
bit too one-sided.'

'You come with me, please,' the Colonel said.
'I take you to your hotel. Then I question these
men we have arrested.'

'I'd like to know what you get out of them,
Colonel, if you can tell me.'

'Why is it you wish to know?'

They were walking towards the car. 'This
business was all arranged,' Corrigan explained.

'Everybody gets the same treatment'

61

He sat beside the Colonel and the car drove away. Then Corrigan told the Egyptian about the two men in the alley, and the dead man still lying there and the mob which was waiting for him when he returned to the street. ' It's obvious,' he ended, ' that the whole thing was planned. They knew when I reached the Old City and they were ready for me. So I'd like to know who planned it and who gave these men their orders.'

Hadrashi smiled. ' I think you know already who it is, Mr Corrigan.'

For a second Corrigan was startled. Names ran through his mind—Ahmed Badri, Hadrashi, Pappadikos. ' The Purple Priest ! ' he said.

The Colonel nodded. ' I think this is right.'

' But why ? And who *is* this Purple Priest ? Incidentally, I thought you didn't believe in him.'

' Oh, I believe. I do not believe this man is a priest, but I believe he is a criminal and that he has kidnapped Mr Oppenheimer. I do not know why he does this. He is the clever one, but, if Allah wills, we get him, and then, *mafeesh*, he is finished.'

' But why does he want to get rid of *me* ? '

Hadrashi stroked his nose. ' This is difficult. You talked of coincidences, Mr Corrigan. These are no coincidences. It seems that any man who seeks the Tomb of Opi is in danger. I do not know the reason for this. It seems that the Tomb of Opi is connected with this Purple Priest.'

' The Priest claims to be Opi himself,' Corrigan reminded the Colonel.

'Yes, but I think we doubt this, unless a man can come back to life after centuries of death. Many strange things happen in my country, but this!' Hadrashi shook his head. 'Mr Oppenheimer looks for this tomb—he is kidnapped, perhaps dead. You say you will seek this tomb—you are attacked.' His voice dropped to a whisper. 'Now I look for it too, but I do it quietly. I tell nobody.'

'I'm still in the hunt, don't forget.' Corrigan smiled. 'I'm still looking for that tomb—and I may be lucky. Beginner's luck, you know.'

'I think you are not the beginner, Mr Corrigan, in matters of this sort. I am glad that you will still search. You openly and I secretly, between us we will find it.'

'And what about your work on *hasheesh* smuggling?'

Hadrashi shrugged. 'That goes on. It will go on until it is ended.' He sat up. 'Tell me, Mr Corrigan, you met Pappadikos?'

Corrigan grinned. 'I met him all right. But I learned nothing from him—in fact he didn't seem too friendly. And speaking of friends, I don't like his. Ahmed Badri was there.'

Hadrashi looked surprised. 'So? Is strange that. They both interest themselves in Ancient Egypt and it may be that is why they meet. Pappadikos is the one man who may know something of this tomb. You must trust him, Mr Corrigan.'

'So you said before,' Corrigan murmured doubtfully.

' One thing again, please. What is it this man in the Old City says as he dies ? '

' I'd asked him about the Tomb of Opi. He was shot. He said, "Rameses, he tells". Then he died.'

The Colonel was nodding and stroking his nose again. ' "Rameses, he tells",' he repeated. ' Is difficult this. I do not know this Rameses.'

' One of your ancient Pharaohs, wasn't he ? '

' Yes, but I think this cannot be the one, unless Rameses, like Opi, has returned to life.' Hadrashi sat up. ' Here is your hotel, Mr Corrigan. Remember, please, to inform me of everything you do and everything you find.' He smiled. ' One more thing. The man you found in the coffin, this brother to Pappadikos, you know how he died ? I tell you. His body was torn and scratched ; his neck was bitten and he was shot.'

Corrigan looked incredulous. ' They really meant to kill him, didn't they ? What's all this about tearing and biting ? D'you mean by an animal of some kind ? '

' I do, as matter of fact. His wounds you did not see because of the mummy wrappings.'

' But what kind of animal ? '

Hadrashi shook his head. ' Our doctors do not know this. They agree that he was killed by a bullet, but a wild animal attacks and wounds him also, and this is before he is shot. But which animal ? ' He shrugged. ' Is another thing for us to think about, Mr Corrigan. Perhaps you have thought of something when I see you again. It will be soon.'

Corrigan left the Egyptian in the car and walked thoughtfully into the hotel. He was thinking about Rameses and wondering what it was that Rameses could tell ; thinking about the brother of Pappadikos whose torn and bleeding body had been shot, and thinking about the men who had wrapped that body in the tight bindings of a mummy.

Chapter V

THE PAPYRUS

Shrimp was up and dressed and sitting by the window when Corrigan went into the room. He looked pale but cheerful.

'Hello, boy,' Corrigan said. 'You feeling better? You were supposed to stay in bed all day.'

'I know, but I was fed up. It's too warm. I can rest here just as well as in bed and a lot more comfortably. Have you had an interesting afternoon?'

Corrigan lowered himself into a chair and grinned. 'Very! You'd have been fascinated.' He gave Shrimp an account of the afternoon. He told him about Pappadikos and his antiques, and Ahmed Badri, about the Old City, the fight in the alley and the mob in the street. He told him about Rameses and the Colonel and about how Pappadikos's brother had died. 'And that's the lot,' he said. 'A very full afternoon, and I can't complain that I've been bored. I wish you had been with me, Shrimp. It might have made things easier. I needed some help.'

Shrimp nodded. 'Next time, Corrigan. They've had me on my own, and now you. Some time they're going to get us together and that should be quite a scrap. You know, there are so many mysteries about this business that I'm dizzy. There's

Geoff, there's this Pappadikos who was mauled by
a tiger, the other Pappadikos who doesn't want to
help, Badri with the dark eyes, this tale about
Rameses, and, of course, the Purple Priest and his
tomb.' He shook his head and smiled shyly. ' Too
much for my brain, I'm afraid.'

Corrigan was gazing round the bedroom.
' Hello ! What's this ? Two beds and my kit in
here. What's the idea ? '

' I had them do it, Corrigan. I had an odd
feeling about things. There's something going on
in this hotel I don't feel very happy about, and it
struck me that it might be a good thing if you and
I weren't separated again. So I've had you moved
into my room. Any objections ? '

Corrigan grinned. ' A good idea ! I think you
have something. They always seem to have a go
at us when we're apart, so from now on we stay
together.' He stood up. ' And now for dinner !
We'll have it in here, I think.'

After dinner Shrimp felt tired and said he would
rest, so Corrigan left him, strolled downstairs and
through the foyer. He glanced at the people who
were sipping coffee and talking with foreign intensity
in the lounge. Then he went outside where it was
cool night. The street lights were glaring beyond
the palms and the insects were flopping around
them. Somewhere above Corrigan's head a neon-
tube buzzed softly. He craved the cool fresh air,
rare in Cairo's early evening before the day's dust
has settled, as rare as water in a hot desert.

After a few minutes he noticed somebody

standing in the shadow of the mimosa bushes at the
corner of the hotel's garden, somebody small and
still who was watching him, and instinctively Corrigan began to move away from the bright lights
which were glaring down on him. Then a boy
stepped out of the shadow and, like a monkey,
came springing up to the foot of the steps below
Corrigan. He was a ragged dirty little street-boy
caked with street-dust, an untidy lively urchin
with a skull-cap on his head and a dash of white
to show where his grin was. He was carrying a
tray piled high with junk.

' You buy curio, *Effendi* ? ' he piped, and a
chuckle bubbled in his throat. ' You buy from
me ? *Baksheesh ?* '

Corrigan grinned back at him. ' I'll buy *you*,'
he said. ' I'll buy you and take you home as a pet.
How would you like that ? '

' You buy curio, *Effendi*.' The boy rummaged
amongst the junk and pulled out of it a little roll
of papyrus. ' You buy this ? Twenty *piastres* ? '
Then he dropped his voice and hissed : ' Pappa
say you buy ! '

For a second Corrigan was startled, and before
he could answer the big Sudanese commissionaire,
his uniform all a-glitter, his black face shining, came
stalking up, muttering in deep-voiced Egyptian.

He waved at the boy. ' *Imshi !* *Y'alla !* ' he
grunted.

' Hold on a minute,' Corrigan said. ' I like this
boy. I'm going to buy something from him.' He
fished a twenty-five *piastre* note from his pocket and

offered it to the lad. The boy's thin fingers clutched it, he thrust the papyrus into Corrigan's hand, gave him a wide grin, spat like a cat at the commissionaire and darted away into the shadows of the murmuring streets. The commissionaire grunted his disapproval and marched away, while Corrigan pushed the little scroll into his pocket and walked back towards the hotel entrance.

Before he reached it a big car came swinging in from the road and stopped. Colonel Hadrashi jumped out of it and ran up the steps.

' 'Evening, Colonel,' Corrigan said quietly.

Hadrashi turned. ' Good evening, Mr Corrigan. Is you that I come to see. Is lucky that I meet you.'

Corrigan nodded. ' I've been getting some fresh air.'

' Is not wise, Mr Corrigan, that you go alone. I, Mustafa Hadrashi, tell you to have care.'

Corrigan smiled. ' Sure. I'll be careful. But things get a bit dull if you spend all your time being careful, don't you think ? Shall we go inside ? '

They went upstairs to sit with Shrimp. The Colonel talked about the heat. Corrigan wondered why Egyptians always complained about the heat of their country. After all, he thought, they've lived here for thousands of years. They should be used to it by now.

' You came to tell us something, Colonel ? ' he asked.

' Yes, Mr Corrigan. I tell you about the men we arrest today, the men who attack you. We find

nothing, Mr Corrigan.' He shook his head.
' Nothing ! Is strange, this. We question them,
alone and together. We have them in the strong
light, we threaten, but nothing ! ' He shrugged.
' Is what I expect.'

' And you've no idea who gave them their
orders ? ' Corrigan asked.

' No idea. They seem not to know. Some of
these men we know already. But yes ! Not good,
these men. Little criminals all of them, bazaar
thieves, footpads. Two are found to have *hasheesh*
on them. But where it comes from ? Where they
get it ? ' He shrugged again. ' Is not known that.
They find it, they say. One of these also is the
man who is shot while you fight him, Mr Corrigan.
He has the cigarettes with *hasheesh* in them, and
our doctors tell me that he smokes these cigarettes.
But that is all. We find no more.'

Corrigan had taken the little roll of papyrus
from his pocket and was turning it over in his hands.

' What's that, Corrigan ? ' Shrimp asked.

' It's a souvenir I bought from a bright and
dirty-faced young urchin. A bit of papyrus, and
an interesting bit too.'

' How much you pay this little thief ? ' Hadrashi
asked.

' Twenty-five *piastres*.'

The Colonel's small eyes glinted darkly. ' Boh !
They are clever, these street-dogs ! It is financiers
they would all be ! You have been robbed, Mr
Corrigan.'

Corrigan was opening the crackling papyrus

carefully and looking at the neat lines of faded hieratic script. ' Think so ? ' he asked with a grin. He was studying the fresh ink of the writing between the lines of the ancient script and reading the words, written in awkward, spidery characters : ' Go to 25a Fuad Street, Suez. Do what he tells. Burn this '. He passed the scroll to Hadrashi. ' I still say it's an interesting piece of papyrus.'

A slow smile wrinkled the Colonel's face as he read the message ; then he passed it to Shrimp who screwed up his eyes as he read it.

' Who sent it ? ' Shrimp asked.

Corrigan didn't answer. He was thinking that the message had satisfied the Colonel, had pleased him even ; yet it was unsigned.

' Who sent it ? ' Shrimp repeated.

Corrigan was watching Hadrashi. ' Maybe the Colonel 'll tell us,' he said quietly.

Hadrashi was surprised. ' You do not know this ? Is only one man who would send a message on papyrus. But one ! ' Then his eyes danced with amusement. ' You are quick, Mr Corrigan. I see now. You wonder how I know who sends a message which bears no name ? '

Corrigan smiled. ' The point did strike me.'

' I tell you.' Hadrashi laughed. ' This message is from Pappadikos. I know it. Only Pappadikos would use papyrus. Is probable that he has no paper. But you say that one of our street-arabs sells you this ? ' Corrigan nodded. ' Then,' Hadrashi continued, ' then this boy works for him.' He laughed again. ' Pappa knows all the street-

arabs. He sends this one to you with a message
on papyrus so that nobody will suspect. Yes?
That is Pappadikos. It is also his writing.'

Corrigan took the scroll from Shrimp. ' You're
quite right. The boy whispered the name
" Pappadikos " to me. But when I talked to
Pappadikos this afternoon he seemed to be rather
unfriendly. How do we know we can trust him? '

' How do you know you can trust anybody? '
Hadrashi asked, and spoke Corrigan's thoughts.
' You want to go on with this, Mr Corrigan, or
you want to go to England? '

' We're going on with this,' Shrimp said. ' We
owe this Purple Priest a thing or two and we're
going to find Geoff Oppenheimer.'

Corrigan grinned at him. ' Listen to the little
fire-eater! ' He turned to the Colonel. ' Yes,
we're going to see this through.'

Hadrashi was stroking his nose. ' It is good.
You help us and we help you. Not long ago you
tell me it is dull if you do not take risks. Take this
risk. Go to Suez. You must trust Pappadikos.
He is strange, that one, strange and mysterious and
clever. But you must trust him. Otherwise '—he
shrugged—' you do not know what to do.'

' Okay,' Corrigan said. ' We'll go tomorrow
morning, if Shrimp's fit. We'll go by road in
Geoff's car. I don't suppose he'll mind and it
might come in handy.' He looked again at the
papyrus. ' According to instructions, I'm supposed
to burn this. How do we manage that in a room
which has no fireplace? '

Hadrashi held out his hand. ' I will take it for you and destroy it.'

Corrigan looked at him and smiled suddenly. ' That's good of you, but I think I'll do what I'm told.' He struck a match and held the corner of the papyrus in the flame. As the ancient stuff, which had originated in the marshes of the Nile centuries earlier, slowly began to burn he dropped it into an ash-tray. ' Instructions carried out,' he said quietly as he watched the scented smoke spiral up into the room. ' And tomorrow we'll complete the job by going to Suez, the object of the exercise being to find Geoff Oppenheimer.'

' Not forgetting the Purple Priest,' Shrimp interrupted.

The Colonel smiled and stood up. ' I go now. I see you some time, but I cannot say when I see you.' His deep-set black eyes took in the pair of them. ' I see you when the—exercise, yes ?—is almost ended.' He smiled at them and turned towards the door. ' Peace be with you,' he said.

After the Colonel had gone Corrigan took off his jacket. ' It's warm,' he said. ' The Colonel seemed very serious.'

' Soulful,' Shrimp suggested.

Corrigan nodded. ' He'll see us when the exercise is almost ended,' he said. ' He knows more than he's told us, does our Colonel. I suppose he looks on us as a couple of amateurs, which is what we are.' He looked at Shrimp. ' And now, my lad, if we're to get away early in the morning, let's go to bed.'

Shrimp tried to sleep. He had been in bed for most of the day and he found it warm and uncomfortably lumpy. He turned over and listened to the street noises of Cairo. Two or three hours later he was still turning over and the street noises had stopped. He was just thinking how quietly Corrigan was sleeping and remembering how Corrigan could be asleep one instant and awake the next when he, too, fell asleep.

He dreamed. There was a light, a bright star, shining in the distance and coming slowly nearer. As it approached it grew larger, until he could see that instead of a star it was the sun, shining with a red-gold light. Now it was very close, and suddenly Shrimp realised that it was the golden sun on the breast of the Purple Priest. He struggled to sit up but he was fastened to the bed and was helpless. He sweated. He gasped for air. Now the Priest was leaning over him and he could see the living wicked eyes in the dead mask. He was suffocating and he tried to shout.

He was awake ; awake and sweating, and he could still hear the sound of his shout dying away and the light of the cold dawn was coming through the open window.

Corrigan was shaking his shoulder and saying, ' You awake, boy ? '

Shrimp swallowed and it wouldn't go down. He sat up and rubbed his eyes. ' I've had the father and mother of all nightmares,' he said, and grinned ruefully.

Corrigan was sitting on the bed. ' What was it about ? '

Shrimp told him. He missed out nothing, and when he remembered the eyes in the mask he began to sweat again.

' I don't know how much of it was dream and how much was fact,' Corrigan said when Shrimp had finished. ' Smell anything ? '

Shrimp sniffed. He tried again and nodded. ' Yes, I can.' There was something stickily sweet in the air. ' Smells like chloroform.'

' It *is* chloroform,' Corrigan said. ' I'll put the light on and you can have a look at our room.'

In the bright light Shrimp could see the wreckage ; drawers on the floor, wardrobe open, suit-cases open and over the floor clothes spilled carelessly. ' What's happened ? ' he asked. ' Have we had a whirlwind in here ? '

' No, we've had a visitor. Somebody broke into our room, chloroformed us and went through our kit.'

Shrimp tried to shake the fog out of his brain. ' But who was it ? How did he get in ? What was he after ? '

' I'll take the last question first. It's my bet he was after that bit of papyrus.' Corrigan stood up. ' Come on, let's check our luggage. I think we'll find that nothing's gone.'

Together they set to work sorting, folding and packing. After a short time the job was done and Corrigan straightened up. ' Anything missing ? ' he asked.

Shrimp shook his head. ' No, my things are okay.'

' Mine too. Even my money's untouched. It's that bit of papyrus he was after. Good thing I destroyed it. You see what this means ? '

' I can see that somebody wanted to know what was written on that papyrus.'

' Sure. And that ought to mean that anybody who *did* know—Pappadikos who wrote it and Hadrashi who read it—wasn't responsible for our visitor. It ought to mean that.'

Shrimp snorted. ' But you're not doubting the Colonel, surely. That's carrying things a bit far.'

Corrigan smiled. ' I'm at the stage where I'm doubting everybody.' He looked towards the window. ' That's the way he went. I came round in time to see him climb over the rail of the balcony. It wasn't light enough to make out any details and I was fuddled anyway, so that by the time I reached the window he had vanished. But I'm not sure how he came in.'

' The same way, surely ? '

Corrigan shook his head doubtfully. ' I don't think so. Come and have a look.'

They walked out on to the little balcony in the cool morning light and leaned over the wrought-iron rail. Theirs was a first-floor room and there was a drop of about fifteen feet to the ground below.

' Nobody would need a parachute to drop from here,' Corrigan said. ' It's easy enough. But how would he climb up ? '

The hotel had a white stucco front. There were no projections, pipes or windows which could be used as foot-holds.

'I dunno,' Shrimp said thoughtfully. 'Nobody could climb that. But if he went out, he must first of all have come in, and if he didn't climb through the window he must have walked through the door.'

Corrigan nodded. 'Right! The door was locked—it's a Yale-type lock—but anybody with a key could have opened it. He came in that way and set to work. Then I started to come round. My bed is near the door and he wouldn't want to pass it, so he came this way.'

They stood on the balcony and looked at the thin vapours hanging about the streets. An early car went past the hotel, its tyres singing on the road.

'I'd like to know who he was,' Corrigan murmured at last.

'Our visitor?   Don't you know?'

Corrigan looked down at Shrimp and saw the sly grin and the tousled hair. 'Do you?' he asked.

Shrimp's grin widened. 'It was the Purple Priest. I saw him.'

Corrigan looked doubtful. 'That's what I meant when I said I didn't know how much of your dream was real. Odd, isn't it?' He turned towards the window. 'Let's get dressed.'

They dressed quietly and thoughtfully. Then Shrimp went to the window again. 'It's broad daylight,' he said. 'The sun's just coming up. What do we do now?'

Corrigan tightened a strap round his suit-case. 'We'll go downstairs and see who's about at this time of day. Then we'll have breakfast, pay our bill and leave. And we'll tell nobody where we're going. What's more, we won't even mention our visitor.'

Chapter VI

THE AMBUSH

THEY left a few hours later, while it was still cool and before the dust woke up, and took the eighty-mile road which draws a straight line across the desert and joins Cairo to Suez.

Very soon they were out of the city and passing through the irrigated fields which the Nile keeps alive. The *fellaheen* who were working in them stopped to watch the big car. Corrigan had the top down and the breeze was cool in his hair. He drove fairly quickly until he came to the sudden desert. There was nothing to show why the desert started at this point : it was simply the place where Egypt stopped being rich watered fields and started being dead dry desert.

Corrigan slowed the car and looked at Shrimp. ' Like it ? ' he asked.

Shrimp still looked pale but his grin was there. ' Terrific ! It's so—so clean ! '

Corrigan gazed across the expanse of valleys and hills and escarpments of moving sand, with the old dead water-courses which occasionally broke suddenly into the smoothness of a sand-slope. Shrimp's right, he thought, it *is* clean ; everything foul blasted away by the sand or buried underneath it.

' You'd wonder where all the sand came from,'

Shrimp was saying. ' It's magnificent ! So still
and quiet, and yet at the same time it's moving
and alive.'

Corrigan nodded. He pulled into the side of
the road and stopped the car. Shrimp's eyes were
shining. He's always the same, Corrigan said to
himself. He never gets over the wonder of things
and admires them enthusiastically. And he's right
again. The sand *is* moving. A light breeze was
blowing from the south, and continuously and
silently the sand grains were rolling and scurrying
across the road in regiments with a living urge to
get to the other side. He looked up at the great
dead dunes beside the road. They were still and
permanent, but the grains were restlessly spilling
over their beetling crests and rolling the desert
invisibly onwards. The moving desert !

From behind them a car came sweeping up the
road, and passed them with its horn blaring and
its tyres spreading panic among the purposeful little
sand grains.

' Well, well,' Corrigan murmured. ' See who
that was ? '

Shrimp looked round. ' No, I was dreaming.
Who was it—Tutankhamen ? '

' No, but somebody who ought to be about the
same age. It was Badri.'

Shrimp's forehead wrinkled. ' Badri ? What's
he up to ? '

' Search me ! When I saw him last, which was
about ten seconds ago, he was making for Suez in
a hurry.'

Shrimp thought this over. Something Corrigan had said was bothering him. ' " Somebody who ought to be about the same age ",' he repeated. ' Tutankhamen ? Badri ? What do you mean, Corrigan ? '

Corrigan was grinning. ' I was just thinking that if Badri's the Purple Priest and the Purple Priest is Opi, as he claims to be, that makes Badri about three thousand five hundred years old. Get it ? '

' I get it.' Shrimp smiled. ' Personally I wouldn't put Badri at more than thirty, but if you say he's as old as Tutankhamen I believe you. How do you know that Badri's the Purple Priest ? '

Corrigan grinned again. ' I don't. I was just thinking it would be nice if he turned out to be. I haven't a clue who the Purple Priest is.'

' Badri gives me the willies. I dislike him so much that I'm sure he won't be the Purple Priest. Notice him this morning when we were leaving ? Bowing and scraping, and hoping we would have a good journey although we hadn't told him where we were going. And those eyes of his ! Cunning, mocking, mysterious ! ' Shrimp shuddered. ' He gives me the creeps.'

Just then another car came rushing along the road from Cairo and left the sand swirling as it disappeared round the bend ahead.

' Hadrashi ! ' Shrimp gasped. ' That was the Colonel ! '

Corrigan nodded and pressed the starter. ' Let's join the procession,' he said.

They bowled along the road and very soon the monotony of the miles made them silent. They passed the ruined Palace of Abbassi, and hummed down the slope into the dried-up Wadi el Gafra without a thought for the mighty river which must have flowed there in the days when it rained in Egypt. Camel thorn grew along the sides of the roads, drawing itself up into little twisted shrubs and living on water which couldn't be there, and on the camel thorn were the snails, and their spiral shells lay in hundreds on the sand where they had fallen in death.

Soon the car came to a straight length of road where the dunes were bigger and were threatening to creep over the tarmac. The car was speeding through a canyon of sand. Suddenly Corrigan swung the wheel over and the Packard lurched across the road and back again in a wide swerve, and Shrimp heard a sharp crack and saw a shadow on top of one of the dunes and smoke drifting up into the sky.

Corrigan pulled the car off the road and came to a slithering broadside stop beside the dunes. ' We're being shot at ! ' he grunted.

They were sheltered by the dunes and now could not see the man who had shot at them. Shrimp smiled. ' He missed,' he said. ' He was up on top of that very big sand-hill. I saw the smoke.'

' I saw the flame,' Corrigan said. ' I happened to be looking. That's why I swerved. Somebody doesn't want us to get to Suez. Let's go and find out who it is.'

He leapt out of the car and Shrimp followed him. They went straight at the nearest sand-slope and started to climb, but the sand avalanched and slithered and made hard going of it, so that by the time they reached the top they were sweating.

Corrigan rested on one knee and looked along the ridge. 'No sign of him,' he muttered. He stood up and sprinted across the ridge in long light strides, and Shrimp came up with him when he stopped after about fifty yards.

Corrigan was staring at a little hollow in the sand at the top of a dune. 'Here's where he was lying,' he said.

Shrimp saw something glinting in the sun and picked it up. 'And here's the cartridge-case,' he said.

Corrigan took it and examined it. 'British. Lee Enfield ·303—Army-type rifle.'

He searched the clean sand at the top of the dune and found a cigarette-end. It was a thin home-made cigarette, stained brown with juice. 'He had a smoke,' Corrigan went on thoughtfully. 'I suppose he'd be a bit fidgety, waiting up here. I'll keep this.' He slipped the stub into the breast pocket of his open-necked shirt and straightened up. 'Now let's get after the dirty little highwayman. You can see his footprints going down the back of this dune.'

He started to move but a gesture from Shrimp stopped him. Shrimp was pointing to the road below, and Corrigan saw that a man had just stepped out from a valley in the sand about two

hundred yards ahead and was now hurrying towards
Suez. He was carrying a rifle over one shoulder
and he walked with a stiff and sideways-swaying
movement.

' That's him ! ' Shrimp said.

Corrigan nodded. ' He's lame. Has a club-
foot. We'll know that joker next time we meet him.
Let's get back to the car. We may catch him.'

As they moved, the man disappeared round a
bend and almost immediately they heard the sound
of a car starting up and racing away.

' Brought his transport with him,' Corrigan
grunted. ' It looks like a well-planned ambush.
Lucky thing they didn't pick a better shot. Whoever planned this job is going to be annoyed with
our limping friend.'

They slid down the slope to the Packard, jumped
into it, and Corrigan started the engine and swung
the car back on to the road. He was driving it
hard and the wind came whistling over the screen.
Shrimp glanced at him and saw the determination
in the mouth and chin and the cold anger in the
eyes. He smiled. Corrigan doesn't like people
who are either too friendly or too hostile, he said
to himself. I suppose being shot at falls into the
too-hostile category.

Soon they came out on to the plain. It was a
brown burnt-up plain, across which stretched pools
of mirage-blue, while here and there dust-devils
whirled themselves into nothingness. In the distance a line of green showed where vegetation grew
beside the Canal, and in front of them the bulk of

Suez rose up, trembling and wavering in the heat.
To the south the leaden smoothness of the Red Sea
stretched away to the sky, and behind them they
could see where a line of blue mountains started
suddenly out of the plain and became lost in the
distant purple haze.

Very soon they were driving along the road
beside the Canal and into Suez, where they quickly
found Fuad Street and parked the car.

'What was the number?' Corrigan asked.
'Was it 25a?'

Shrimp nodded. 'It's here,' he said. 'We've
stopped right in front of it.'

They were looking at another antique shop, like
the one in Cairo only smaller and dustier and less
interesting. They went inside.

Behind the counter a man was seated on a stool.
He was a little old man, dressed in the flowing
garments of the East, and he was smoking a hookah
which gurgled as he drew the cool smoke through
it. A wisp of white beard shone around his chin.
He didn't look up.

Corrigan tapped the counter. 'My name's
Corrigan,' he said. 'I was told to come here.'

The gurgling went on, and the man spoke
without taking the tube from his mouth and without looking up. 'You go Hotel Splendide. You
wait. He tells you what you do.'

'Who's "he"?' Corrigan asked.

The hookah spluttered while Corrigan waited
but nothing happened. He grinned down at
Shrimp. 'Talkative bloke, isn't he? Let's go.'

They left the shop and drove along Fuad Street and found the Hotel Splendide at the top of it. It was a small quiet hotel, with a French manager who welcomed them with a lot of fussy bowing and over-done politeness. He had the moustache and goatee beard of the cartoon Frenchman, and his conversation was full of ' *M'sieur* ', ' *Oui* ' and ' *Voila* '.

' He looks too French to be true,' Shrimp commented as he sat on one of the beds in the small clean room they had taken. ' I think he puts on an act—exaggerates his Frenchness.'

' I hope he isn't the one Methuselah said would tell us what to do,' Corrigan said, smiling. ' If he is, it 'll take him a week to tell us, and by the time he's finished it 'll be too late to do it.'

After lunch Corrigan and Shrimp sat in the small lounge of the hotel. It was cool and pleasant, and Shrimp, tired by the morning's journey, was lolling back in a chair with his eyes closed when Corrigan nudged him. He jerked himself upright. ' What's up ? ' he asked.

Corrigan was grinning. ' Here comes Alphonse with " at your service " running out of his ears.'

The little French manager bounced across the lounge like a ball. He looked at Corrigan. ' *M'sieur!* There is a gentleman who would speak with you.'

Corrigan stretched his long legs and rocked his chair backwards. ' Who is he, Alphonse ? '

The Frenchman shrugged. ' That I cannot say, *m'sieur*. *C'est impossible*. He is in the garden on the roof and he waits.'

(1,824) 7

'Ask him to come down then.'

Alphonse pursed his lips and looked sad. 'He is the old one this, *m'sieur*. He is '—he spread his hands—'he is obese—fat.'

'Okay,' Corrigan said, and levered himself up out of his chair. 'I don't want to move, but my curiosity gets the better of me.'

Alphonse stepped back. There was something in Corrigan's size and in his leisurely power which awed the Frenchman. He stepped back like a rabbit dodging from beneath the feet of a race-horse.

Corrigan and Shrimp went up in the lift and walked out on to the roof of the hotel, which was flat and dotted with many potted palms and painted tables under bright canvas sunshades. At first the place seemed deserted, until Corrigan saw where the arms of a man were spilling over the sides of a chair near the edge of the roof. He sauntered across with Shrimp.

As they approached the chair they heard a voice, a bad-tempered grumbling voice. 'We meet again, my big Engleeshman.'

Corrigan grinned. 'Sure thing, Mr Pappadikos. Another coincidence, I suppose?'

'I do not know this "coincidence". Do not use the long words with me.' The Greek, his roundness, his shining face, his little buried eyes and his big moustache, all unchanged, was lying back in a chair beneath a canvas awning. He looked at Shrimp. 'So this is your little friend, with the curling hair and the clean skin.' He nodded. 'I like him.' He gazed across the roofs

of the city and pointed. ' I bring you here to show
you that. Jebel Ataka ! '

They looked over Suez to where the plain
stretched away inland, until it stopped suddenly in
a great wall of jagged rock a thousand feet or more
in height. In the afternoon heat it was shadowy-
black and trembling.

' Jebel Ataka ! ' Pappadikos repeated. ' Fierce
wild mountains where nothing lives. That cliff you
see is several miles from here, but when you reach
it you find that it is rough, broken, with many
ravines running into it.'

Corrigan sat down. ' And what makes you
think we're likely to reach it ? '

Pappadikos looked at him while appearing to
look past him. ' You reach it tomorrow in the
auto of the American.' He smiled. ' Come, my
big friend, let us help each other, you and I. We
work for the same thing.'

' You don't say. Why, what are *you* working
for ? '

' I ? I have a friend. I help him. He looks
for the men who sell *hasheesh*.'

' Colonel Hadrashi ? ' Shrimp said.

The Greek nodded. ' He is my friend. You
look for the American and you look for the Tomb of
Opi.' He sat up and leaned towards them. ' I
tell you. You seek the Tomb of Opi. I help my
friend the Colonel of Police and I also find the
murderer of my brother—him you find in the
ancient coffin. Yes ? I think we work together.'
He pointed at Corrigan. ' You, big Engleeshman,

you find the first thing that leads us to the Tomb
of Opi. You remember what the man say—the
one who is shot ? '

' " Rameses, he tells ".'

Pappadikos nodded. ' That is right. This
Rameses was a king of Old Egypt. Many, many
centuries are gone since he die. He has a statue
in the Temple of Amun at Thebes, but I think this
is not the one the man means. You know what I
think ? I tell you. I think that somewhere in the
Jebel '—he pointed towards the distant mountains
—' is a rock which looks like this Rameses, and
that where the rock is you find the Tomb of Opi.'
He shrugged. ' It may not be a rock-shape : it
may be a picture on the rock, but it will be something. I think you go tomorrow to look for this
rock. No ? '

Corrigan grinned. ' I wouldn't be surprised if
you were right. You know something else ? You're
not the only one who knows we're looking for the
tomb.'

' No ? You tell me, please.'

Corrigan told him about the ambush on the
Suez road and described the man with the club-
foot.

Pappadikos bobbed up and down in his chair.
His eyes danced with excitement. ' That one I
know ! That is Abdul the Lame. We get him and
make him talk. Oh, yes, Abdul will talk. This is
good, my friends. We have something, but say
nothing of this. I will deal with Abdul.'

' You haven't found him yet,' Shrimp said.

'No, but soon I have. Today—tomorrow— soon.'

'If you *can* find him,' Corrigan said. He took the cigarette-stub from his pocket and handed it to the Greek. 'He left this behind on top of a dune.'

Pappadikos took it and held it between a fat finger and thumb. He sniffed at it and then pulled it apart. ' *Hasheesh!* ' he said. 'This one also is a drug-smoker.' He shook his head slowly. 'Everything leads to *hasheesh*. It is a wicked thing, this drug they get from the good hemp, my friends, and we must stop it.'

'Who?' Shrimp asked. 'You and the Colonel?'

Pappadikos was nodding and looking at them from beneath his half-closed eyelids. 'Yes, that is right. And you, also, you help.'

'How?' Corrigan asked. 'What have we to do with dope smugglers?'

'You will see. Now listen to Pappa. I think you are not new to danger, my big friend?'

Corrigan grinned. 'We've been in a few spots.'

'*Aiwa!* It is as I think. You are in danger now, and tomorrow when you go to the Jebel the danger is greater. You will have care. I, Pappa, will watch for you. You will not see me but I shall be near.' He had been talking earnestly. Now he paused and his eyes twinkled darkly. 'We make the plan. If you need help you come for Pappa. If one of you is captured the other comes for help. If it is evening you come to the roof of this hotel—I am always here in the evening looking towards the Jebel—and you find me. If it is

daytime you go to the shop at the end of this street
—where you go today—and you say'—he laughed
suddenly and they saw his small white teeth—' you
say, " Pappa, your children need help ".   Yes ? '

Corrigan grinned back at him.   ' Okay, Pappa.'

They heard the whirring of the lift and a second
later the manager stepped out on to the roof.   He
came towards them and Corrigan noticed how he
glanced, almost in fear, at Pappadikos.

' *M'sieur* Corrigan,' he said.   ' There is one who
would see you below.   Another gentleman.'

' We seem to be getting popular,' Corrigan
murmured.   ' Is this gentleman also old and fat ? '
he asked with a smile.

The Frenchman shrugged. ' Old, *m'sieur* ? *Mais
non*.   Fat ?   Hm !   So, so.'

' Okay,' Corrigan said, ' we'll go, if you'll excuse
us, Mr Pappadikos.'

Pappadikos smiled, and as they left they heard
him tell the manager to bring some aniseed.   They
went down in the lift and walked into the lounge.
A man was standing at a window.   He turned
when he heard them and there was a silent moment
while they stared at him.   It was Ahmed Badri, in
light-grey suit, swelling in the middle, and red
tarboosh, his deep eyes hidden by sun-glasses.

He smiled.   ' Mr Corrigan !   Mr Bradley !   I
did not think to see you again so soon.'

' No,' Corrigan said quietly.   ' I didn't think
so either.'

' How did you know we were here ? ' Shrimp
asked.

'Everybody knows where everybody is in this town,' Badri answered with a shrug. 'That is Suez. I bring you this.' He held out a camera in a leather case. 'It is found in your room after you leave this morning, and as it does not belong to the hotel it must belong to you.'

'I suppose it must,' Corrigan said, still very quietly. His brain was working quickly. He was wondering what was behind this, and whether to let Badri make all the moves or to tackle him directly and shake the truth out of him. 'I suppose it must,' he repeated and took the camera. 'Nice of you to bring it all the way from Cairo.'

'But I must come to Suez, Mr Corrigan,' the Egyptian explained. 'I am often in Suez. Here I have interests also.'

'I wouldn't be surprised,' Shrimp muttered.

Badri turned to go. 'I hope you enjoy your stay here. It is an interesting town, but, pah! it smells. It is also too far from the things of Ancient Egypt. Cairo is more beautiful. Perhaps we meet again, Mr Corrigan.'

'And that wouldn't surprise me either,' Corrigan said, and watched the broad-shouldered Egyptian go through the door.

Shrimp sat down. 'Surprise!' he said. 'Still, it was nice of him to bring you the camera. I didn't know you had one, Corrigan.'

Corrigan was looking at the camera in his hands. It was an expensive instrument in a case of brown leather. 'Neither did I,' he answered.

Shrimp sat up. 'It isn't yours then? Well, why on earth didn't you tell him?'

'I had the feeling he already knew. I think we were intended to have this, and I'm wondering why.' Corrigan was turning the camera over in his big hands. He unfastened the flap of the case and very gently slid the camera out and a piece of paper fluttered to the carpet. Corrigan picked it up and, as he read it, Shrimp saw his eyes go cold and narrow.

'Come here, boy,' Corrigan said. 'Take a look at this.'

Shrimp stood up and took the paper. It was cheap scented notepaper, with words printed on one side of it. He read them aloud. ' " Opi, Chief Priest of Amun-Ré, warns all who violate his eternal habitation that they will die ".' He stood in thought for a moment and then he smiled. 'I've heard that before. What d'you think the idea's supposed to be, Corrigan?'

Corrigan was looking at the camera. 'It's a beauty is this,' he was saying. 'Why should he just give it away?' He took the camera to the window and turned it over thoughtfully. 'I get it,' he nodded. 'It has the initials " G.O." scratched on the bottom of it. That mean anything to you, young Bradley?'

'Geoff Oppenheimer,' Shrimp suggested.

'Right! Geoff Oppenheimer it is. You ask what the idea is. It's the old idea they've tried before—they're trying to scare us.' Corrigan grinned. 'But we don't scare so easily, do we, boy?'

Shrimp smiled. ' I think *they* must be getting scared.'

' I think you're right. But I can't imagine what we've done to scare them—yet. I'll tell you something else about this camera. Geoff didn't have it with him when we went to the Pyramids the other night.'

' No ! ' Shrimp whispered. ' You're dead right, Corrigan. Therefore it must have been pinched.'

Corrigan nodded. ' It must have been pinched from his room at the hotel, either by Badri or by somebody who had access to Geoff's room and who put it in our room after we'd left. Somebody who worked in the Oasis Hotel.'

' Do we tell Pappa ? ' Shrimp asked.

Corrigan thought for a short time. ' I don't think so. The old wizard seems to know everything. Let's keep this one to ourselves.' He pushed the camera into his pocket. ' Now let's go up to our room and sort out our kit. Then we'll fill the car up with petrol and we're all set for an early start in the morning.'

CHAPTER VII

THE RAVINE

THEY had breakfast early the next morning and then went to pack their rucksacks.

' We may be out there in the wilds for two or three days,' Corrigan said. ' Water's going to be the problem. We've a bottle each : we'll have to ration it.'

' It isn't water I'm worrying about,' Shrimp grumbled. ' It's food. Dates, cheese, chocolate and biscuits ! For two or three days ! I'll probably shrivel up and blow away.'

Corrigan grinned. ' You're shrivelled already, small fry. Now get cracking. We want to be well on our way before the day gets hot.'

There was a polite tap on the door and the manager bowed himself into the room. His eyes were puffed with sleep and his beard was uncombed. He looked troubled and hesitant, like a child about to tell his teacher that there is a mistake in the sum on the blackboard.

' *M'sieur,*' he murmured.

Corrigan straightened up. ''Morning, Alphonse. What's wrong ? Get it off your chest.'

' *M'sieur,* it is often that our guests collect curios —but this one ! '

Shrimp scratched his head. His face was shining with early-morning fitness and his little shy smile

was there again. 'Now, Alphonse,' he said en-
couragingly, 'take a deep breath and start again.
We don't know what you're talking about.'

Alphonse's hands fluttered. 'But, *m'sieur*! The
men, they bring it. It rests in the foyer and I
cannot leave it there. My other guests! What
will they think?' His eyes rolled up to the ceiling.

'And how do you know it's ours?' Corrigan
asked.

'The men say for *M'sieur* Corrigan.'

'And what is it?'

Alphonse smiled indulgently. 'You joke, *m'sieur*.
The English joke always. I have it brought up to
your room, and when you return from your journey
you make the arrangements for it. But it is so
heavy!'

'But what is it?' Shrimp asked.

'It's okay,' Corrigan said. 'Send it up,
Alphonse.'

In a few minutes the Frenchman was back and
he opened the door wide. He was followed by two
hefty Sudanese, who grunted as they staggered
under the weight of a large Ancient Egyptian coffin
which they lowered carefully to the carpet.

Shrimp stared at it. Its lid was covered with
old designs and hieroglyphs in faded colours, while
the formalised figure of an Ancient Egyptian, naked
except for a kilt, and standing with the rigidity of
centuries, was painted on one end of it.

Corrigan's voice had gone cold and even.
'Who brought it?' he was asking.

'The men, *m'sieur*,' Alphonse answered.

' Which men ? Where were they from ? Where did they go ? '

' I know not, *m'sieur*.' Alphonse threw up his hands. ' The men were Egyptians. I have not seen them before. They were dirty Egyptians of the bazaars. They bring in this '—he pointed to the coffin—' they say it is for you and they go away in an automobile.'

' Did you see their car ? '

' No, *m'sieur*. I hear it.'

Corrigan nodded thoughtfully. ' Would you know them again ? '

' *Mais non*, *m'sieur*.' Alphonse shrugged. ' I do not look at them.'

' Right, Alphonse.' Corrigan walked to the coffin and knelt down on one knee beside it. He looked up. The two Sudanese had left, the door was closed and Alphonse and Shrimp were watching him, Shrimp with keyed-up expectancy, Alphonse with a hint of disapproval in his eyes.

' I'm going to open this coffin,' Corrigan said slowly. ' You're going to get a shock, an unpleasant one, so be ready.'

He lifted the lid gently, and then suddenly pushed it off and let it slide on to the carpet. Alphonse gasped, squeaked and sat quickly down on the bed. Shrimp whistled softly and bent over the coffin. He was looking at the body of a man, a dark-skinned man from whose face evil had been driven ; driven out by the terror of the death which had claimed him.

Corrigan was nodding and smiling his relief.

'I thought it was going to be Geoff,' he said.
'You recognise him, Shrimp ? '

'Yes,' Shrimp answered quietly. He was looking at the man's twisted leg. 'It's Abdul the
Lame.'

'Right. It's Abdul the Lame, the man who
couldn't shoot. He won't be shooting any more,
poor devil.'

'But what's happened to him ? ' Shrimp was
staring at the dead man's face and neck which were
torn and bitten. 'What killed him ? '

Corrigan stood up. 'You remember the other
one—Pappa's brother ? He was wrapped up in
yards of linen ; this one isn't. But remember what
Hadrashi said about how he died ? He'd been
savaged by an animal of some kind. So's this chap.
But the animal didn't kill him.' He bent down
again and pointed. 'That did.' He was pointing
to a small hole in the man's jacket over the heart ;
a hole into which black blood had soaked like ink
into blotting-paper. 'He was shot,' Corrigan
ended, and stood up again.

'But why ? ' Shrimp asked. 'And why send
him to us ? '

'I think I know,' Corrigan answered quietly.
'He was killed because he failed to kill us and
because he was so easily recognised. Therefore he
was dangerous. He was sent to us as another
warning. They're still trying to scare us, boy.'

'And are we scared ? '

Corrigan didn't answer for a moment. There
was no need. The answer was in his face, in the

cold dangerous eyes and the firm purposeful mouth and chin. ' No, we aren't scared,' he said at last. ' Speaking for myself I'm beginning to get annoyed, and I think it's time I went after this Purple Priest.'

' You think that's who it is ? '

' Must be. The Priest was connected with the first murder. He must be connected with this one because of the method and the coffin.' Corrigan turned to the manager who was still sitting on the bed, his head in his hands, moaning. ' Buck up, Alphonse,' he said. ' You aren't being very helpful.'

' My hotel, m'sieur, my hotel. The police will come.'

Corrigan nodded. ' Sure. And you couldn't have more respectable people. Is M'sieur Pappa-dikos in the hotel ? '

' Oui, m'sieur. He sleeps late.'

Corrigan put a hand on the Frenchman's shoulder and with no apparent effort raised the little man to his feet. ' Right. You go and get him. Tell him we've found Abdul the Lame for him. Tell him everything—how this coffin was brought to the hotel and how we opened it. On your way.'

Alphonse, still moaning and rolling his eyes upwards, went slowly out of the room and, as the door closed behind him, Corrigan picked up his rucksack. ' Grab your things, Shrimp,' he said. ' Let's go ! '

Shrimp looked startled. ' Go ? ' He pointed to the body in the coffin. ' But what about this ? '

' Leave him for Pappa. We can't do anything about him, and if we hang around here until the police come we'll be here for the rest of the day, and we have things to do.'

Shrimp drove the Packard while Corrigan studied the map. It was early and Suez was still quiet ; they slipped out of it almost stealthily. After a few miles they left the road and set off across the open desert straight for one end of Jebel Ataka. Soon they came to a place where bits of rusted angle-iron stuck out of the sand with lengths of old barbed-wire twisted about them, and the level monotony of firm sand was broken by tyre-tracks imprinted years before.

' An old army camp,' Corrigan said, and pointed to a heap of battered brown tins.

Jebel Ataka was nearer now. They could see the jagged immensity of it as it towered into the sky, but it was another hour before they were close enough to see how the cliff-face was dissected and split into numberless ravines separated by spires and knife-edges of sharp rock. Corrigan was so fascinated by the harsh beauty of the sight that he forgot why they were there. He knew that torrents must have poured down those mountains in the days, thousands of years ago, when rain came to that part of Egypt. Now the rain never comes and the rivers have gone, but the canyons and gorges they left are still there, savage and unsmoothed, and hot under the sun.

In low gear the Packard was climbing a long slope of pebbles which fanned out for a mile or more from the base of the cliff, and occasionally it slipped and skidded on the round stones. Shrimp's face was wrinkled with concentration, but his small hands on the wheel never lost their control. As they came near to the Jebel the pebbles became smaller and the bed of them thicker so that the big car began to flounder. Then they drove into the shadow of a boulder and Shrimp stopped the car.

' Engine's getting hot,' he said. ' We can't drive much farther on this surface. What shall we do ? '

Now that the car had stopped, the heat-waves from the sun-lit rock around them came rolling up and a few flies buzzed hopefully about.

' We'll leave her here,' Corrigan said. ' I'd hoped that we might have been able to drive along the base of the cliff and explore it from the car, but we'll have to walk. And there's something like fifty miles of it according to the map.' He picked up his rucksack and climbed out of the car.

Shrimp groaned and followed him. ' Fifty miles on these pebbles ! It's like Brighton Beach, only more so. It's going to take days, Corrigan.'

' I know. I also know that we're going to do it.'

' If you say so, but it seems crazy to me. We've rations for three days, so we'll have to walk for a day and a half and then come back to the car, by which time we'll be out of grub. What do we do then ? Go back to Suez for more, and then out to the point we'd reached and on for another day and a half? '

' That's the way we'll do it.'

Shrimp looked disgusted. ' But it's going to take a fortnight, Corrigan.'

'I know. There's an alternative if you want it. I'll walk along the cliff for three days while you stay with the car and drive back to the sand and along to the point I've reached to pick me up. That way we'd do it in half the time.'

'Oh, no! You're not getting away with that!' Shrimp shook his head in a determined way. 'Where you go, I go. What I'm getting at is this, Corrigan. Is it worth it? I'd certainly like to see the Tomb of Opi, but is it worth all the energy? Isn't there another way?'

Corrigan shook his head slowly. 'I don't think so. We're in this now, son, up to the ears, and I think this tomb is the key to the whole thing. We must find it. In fact we're going to find it, and this is the only way.' Corrigan grinned suddenly. 'Cheer up! We may find it in the first hour. Don't forget we have something to help us.'

Shrimp snorted. 'You mean old Rameses? "Rameses, he tells",' he mimicked in a squeaky voice. 'Well, I hope the old buffer's looking out for us. Come on, let's get started.'

They began to walk. Shrimp could now look about him, and he was soon thrilled by the towering hostility of the Jebel and by the harshness of the jagged rock. 'It's terrific!' he whispered, and Corrigan smiled when he saw Shrimp's eyes shining with excitement and wonder. He's okay, he said to himself. It's not like Shrimp to start grumbling at the beginning of a job; must still be feeling the effects of that crack on the head.

They walked for a couple of hours until the heat of the sun burning down on them and thrown back at them by acres of stone began to make Shrimp feel dizzy. He walked into the shade of a big needle of rock and plumped down on a boulder. ' I'm faint from lack of food,' he muttered, ' and I simply *must* have a drink. If I don't I'm likely to dry up and be wafted away.'

Corrigan squatted down beside him and opened his rucksack, and they began to eat biscuits and dates. They allowed themselves a good mouthful each of the water from one of the bottles, and fought against the temptation to empty the contents of the bottle down their throats. Shrimp soon revived, and after the food he wiped his face and leaned back against the rock. He saw that they had stopped in the mouth of one of the many ravines which cut into the Jebel, and he could follow its twisting course for about twenty yards until a bend hid the rest of it. It was a place where it seemed that man had never been before and had no right to be now ; an eerie and awesome place in which nothing lived ; a narrow canyon with a pebbly bottom and towering walls of rough untamed rock, all baking in the sun. It had a hot dustiness about it and, although there was no smell of death, there was instead a complete absence of life. Even the flies had left it and there was no camel-thorn growing.

Shrimp shuddered. ' This place doesn't like us,' he whispered.

Corrigan nodded. He knew that Shrimp was

feeling the hostility of the rock. ' It 'll have to get used to us,' he said.

' But can't you feel it, Corrigan? Can't you feel that something is watching us and hating us all the time, wherever we go ? '

' Yes, I get the feeling. It's brought on by the loneliness and the silence.'

' Possibly. But it's queer, isn't it ? Like prowling round the enemy camp in the middle of the night.'

Corrigan smiled at the intensity of the excitement in Shrimp's face. ' Don't let your imagination work overtime. There's nothing here but rock.'

' There is. There's Opi's tomb somewhere. Incidentally we don't seem to have done so much searching so far. Speaking for myself, I don't even know what to look for, and if I did I wouldn't know where to look. The tomb could be up any of these ravines which cut into the cliff, and we must have passed at least a dozen of them already. To do the job properly we ought to search every one.'

' Sure, but it would take years. I'm staking everything on finding this statue of Rameses, or whatever it is. I've a healthy respect for that wise old bird Pappadikos, and he guesses that there'll be a rock somewhere that looks like Rameses. When we find it we go up the ravine nearest to it.'

Shrimp nodded thoughtfully. ' So we ought to start studying rocks ? '

' I've been studying them ever since we started.'

'And what about the tomb? What do you think that's going to look like?'

Corrigan scratched his head. 'Search me. I'm no Egyptologist. I suppose it 'll be a hole in the rock.'

'Pity Geoff isn't here,' Shrimp said. 'He'd have been a big help.'

'I think when we find the tomb we'll find Geoff as well.'

Shrimp's eyebrows went up. 'You think they have him in the tomb? In that case we *must* find it.'

Corrigan nodded. 'That's what I've been trying to tell you. We're going to find it.' He was talking in that quiet confident way of his. 'Everything depends on it. For some reason this tomb's important—that's why they've made so many attempts to scare us off. That's why they kidnapped Geoff.' He grinned suddenly. 'What they can't understand is that they're simply making us more curious than ever.' He stood up and stretched. 'Ready, boy? Let's go.'

They plodded on through the afternoon. Shrimp studied every projecting rock in an attempt to find one that looked like an Egyptian king, until he was beginning to see all kinds of unlikely shapes in the tortured rocks. Corrigan appeared to be glancing about him lazily through half-closed eyes. He was missing nothing.

Gradually the sun moved into the western sky and blue-black shadows began to appear on the great cliffs. These grew steadily, until the lofty ridges at the top of the Jebel went purple and sent long shadows across the desert towards the Red Sea.

'Time we were finding a spot to make camp for the night,' Corrigan said.

'Camp?' Shrimp said with a grin. 'Where's the tent and what do we use for a bed?'

'We don't need a tent and these pebbles 'll do for a bed. What we need is a sheltered spot near to the rock where we'll be warm.' Corrigan stopped and looked back at Shrimp. 'What's wrong?' he asked.

Shrimp was staring across the level sea of pebbles that stretched away from the Jebel towards the Red Sea. 'Funny,' he murmured and pointed. 'Look over there, Corrigan. In this light you can get the impression that there's a track running across this scree from the direction of Suez.'

Corrigan looked. He looked to where the great dead delta merged with the desert and the gathering haze. It was a brown monotony, broken by a broad strip which came up out of the distance and made straight for the Jebel. It was grey and smooth. 'Of course!' Corrigan whispered. 'Why didn't I think of it before? It's obvious!' He grinned. 'Good for you, Shrimp! You keep your eyes open. I wouldn't have seen it.'

'You think it *is* a track?'

Corrigan nodded. 'Sure of it. If people come to this tomb they must come by car. These pebbles wouldn't show tyre-tracks so they think they'd be safe. But the tyres would alter the " lie " of the pebbles—make them all lie flat—and that would have an effect on the amount of light reflected from them. It would have stuck out a mile on an air photo.'

Shrimp looked again at the track. 'So you think that a car has come across there and that that's the way to the tomb?' He shook his head. 'I can't think why.'

'It's obvious, boy. If the Purple Priest comes to the tomb it must be because he uses it for something. That's why he's so keen on stopping anybody who tries to find it. If he comes he uses a car, in spite of the fact that he claims to be Opi and a few thousand years old.' Corrigan nodded towards the track. 'That's the result. Evidently a track that a car *can* keep on. He's probably travelled across there scores of times. Let's go and have a look.'

They hurried forward for about a hundred yards. When they reached the track it was impossible to see any difference between the pebbles on it and those on each side. Shrimp stood gazing towards where he could see the track very definitely coming from the direction of Suez and followed it to the point, some distance in front of him, where it melted into the desert of stones at his feet.

Corrigan was walking about, searching, and suddenly he squatted down and called to Shrimp. When Shrimp reached him he was pointing at a flat brown pebble, larger than the average, on which was a darker-brown oval mark. 'Seen anything like that before?' Corrigan asked.

Shrimp crouched. His eyes were sparkling with excitement. 'Yes, on roads at home in summer. You can find plenty of these marks on the dry tarmac. They're caused by oil dripping from moving cars.'

Corrigan was smiling at him, enjoying his boyish excitement. ' Right ! You'll only find a mark like that where a car has been. And if you draw a line through the length of it, it points the way the car was going. See where this one points ? '

They stood up slowly and faced the towering cliffs. They were looking at the mouth of another ravine. It was narrower than the average, and its walls were straight and smooth where they had been polished by centuries of rushing water. Now they were dry and dead.

' That's it,' Corrigan whispered. ' Let's go.'

As soon as they entered the ravine it bent to the right and they were in a straight length of about fifty yards. The floor which was level and pebbly sloped upwards steadily, and the perpendicular walls were about thirty feet high. They grew quickly higher. The little breeze from the plain outside never reached inside the ravine, and the air was still and silent. The crunch of their shoes on the pebbles echoed about loudly. The sun was on the highest crests of the Jebel in front of them.

The hot dry silence of the place affected Shrimp quickly. His heart thumped as he tried to walk quietly on the pebbles. He had the feeling that he was being watched. He glanced back over his shoulder, gasped and swung round. ' Corrigan ! ' he croaked.

Corrigan turned. He was looking back at the flat wall of the ravine which hid the plain from view. The long shadows from the crags and rock-pinnacles behind them were creeping down the cliffs and one of them had fallen on the wall. It was shaped like the head of a man, in full face. He had the bobbed hair of the Ancient Egyptian and from his forehead rose a snake, while some uneven quality in the rock gave the uncanny impression of features—stern mouth and slanting watchful eyes.

'Rameses!' Corrigan said quietly. 'Well, we've found him. He's just a queer shadow-effect—if you didn't happen to be here at this time of day you'd never see him.' He was speaking his thoughts, a thing he often did when there was only Shrimp to hear them. 'So that settles it! This *is* the ravine. We've found it and on the first day. All we have to do now is find the tomb.' He nodded. 'We'll have to go carefully. Ready, boy?'

They walked forward. They were climbing steadily into the trapped heat inside the ravine which had a heavy burning quality. At each bend, and there were many of them, Corrigan stopped, pressed himself against the rock and peered cautiously forward before going on.

Shrimp kept close behind him. The gloom in the ravine, the silence and the immensity of the great cliffs which were slowly shutting out the sky, made him feel tiny and unimportant, like an ant in a maze.

They had gone about a mile into the heart of the Jebel when Corrigan paused at a bend, looked forward and then turned to Shrimp. The cold glint of his eyes and the straight line of his mouth told Shrimp that their search was over.

' Rameses ! '

Shrimp's heart thumped wildly as he leaned forward to look. What he saw ahead of them and in the opposite wall of the ravine was a square black opening. He turned to Corrigan. ' That's it, I suppose ? ' he whispered.

Corrigan nodded. ' I want to get nearer to it. I think we can manage it without being seen.'

The ravine had widened considerably by this time, and the bottom of the cliffs was cracked and broken and large pieces of rock had split away and lay on the pebbles. Corrigan squeezed himself between the cliff and a big boulder, and with Shrimp behind him made his way for about twenty yards until he came out on a ledge about ten feet above the floor of the ravine and nearer to the tomb. They crouched behind a piece of rock which jutted up in front of them and peeped over it.

The tomb entrance was an opening in the cliff about seven feet high. At the base it was six feet wide and its straight even sides sloped inwards slightly. It was a black tunnel inside which nothing moved and in which nothing seemed to have moved for centuries. They watched it in silence for some time.

Then Corrigan turned to Shrimp. ' I'm going in there, boy,' he said. ' You go back the way we came and make for the Packard at top speed. When you find it drive for Suez and get Pappadikos. Tell him we've found the tomb and leave the rest to him. I think you'll find that he'll be out here as fast as a car can bring him.'

One glance at Corrigan's face told Shrimp that

argument was useless. He smiled, his shy nervous smile. 'Okay. But I don't like it.'

Corrigan put a hand on his shoulder. 'Neither do I. But I think it's the only way. There should be a bright moon soon after it gets dark, and that won't be long now, so I think you'll be able to travel pretty quickly. I reckon we came seven or eight miles from the car, but we weren't travelling very fast because we were searching. You'll go a lot faster and, allowing you time for the moon to get up, I think you ought to be back at the car in three hours. I expect Pappadikos to be out here at first light tomorrow. I don't think you've an easy job. It's going to be lonely and a bit spooky, but you'll do it. It's nothing to that trip you did in the jungle not very long ago.'

Shrimp snorted. 'It isn't *that* I don't like, you big dope. It's leaving you.'

Corrigan grinned at him. 'I'll be okay. When you get back here you'll probably find me curled up asleep and the tomb empty.'

He took a torch from his pocket. 'Here we go. I'll see you in the morning, and the best of luck !'

'You're the one who's going to need the luck,' Shrimp hissed after him, as Corrigan dropped from the ledge to the floor of the ravine. Shrimp watched him walk, in that leisurely and deceptive way of his, to the black square which was the Tomb of Opi.

Corrigan didn't pause. He walked straight through the opening and vanished in the darkness.

Chapter VIII

THE CAT

It was gloomy inside the tomb, but enough light came in through the entrance to enable Corrigan to inspect the place once his eyes had focused. It was empty except for four bales of cotton-wool which were lying along one wall. Raw cotton, Corrigan said to himself. What would that be doing here ?

The entrance hall was rectangular and in the wall at the far end of it were two doors, one in each corner, while in front of the wall and between the doors was a dais about a foot high. The doors were massive and old, but not old enough, Corrigan decided, but there was nothing false about the carving in low relief on the wall. It was the carved figure of a man who sat facing the entrance. On his head was a tall helmet and on his breast the circle of the sun, while from above him the sun's rays spread downwards to form a background. The smaller figures of other men, naked from the waist, bowed at his feet. His face expressed scorn and aristocratic pride.

Corrigan walked slowly nearer. ' So that must be Opi,' he whispered, ' the Chief Priest they buried here centuries ago.' The carving fascinated him. The old craftsman had made the rock live, had caused it to express human emotions, so that the eyes which looked down at Corrigan looked at him with hatred. ' Not a nice man,' Corrigan went on, ' to have been feeling as sour as that for thousands of years.'

Then a commotion in the entrance caused him to jump round in time to see a big car swing in through the doorway with headlights blazing. For a second he stood still and the lights threw his shadow at the feet of Opi. He could see little behind the lights, but he knew that the car was filling the entrance so he turned and made for the door in the left-hand corner of the hall. Before he reached it the door opened and a man stood there, a man dressed like a Chief Priest of Ancient Egypt. Corrigan looked at the long purple robe with a golden sun on the breast, at the tall golden helmet and the golden mask with the hooked curving nose and the living eyes glinting in the slits. The Purple Priest ! he said to himself.

He stood still and grinned. ' I've just been having a look at your picture on the wall,' he said. ' It's a pretty good likeness. You're Opi, the bloke who died a few thousand years ago. I'm pleased to meet you. I'm the King of Siam.' He was still grinning, but his eyes were calmly calculating the chances of making a dash for the other door.

' I am Opi, Chief Priest of Amun-Ré,' the Priest was saying. His voice was soft and muffled by the mask and it sounded false. ' All who violate my eternal habitation must die.'

Corrigan scratched his head. ' I've heard that before somewhere,' he said.

Then the Priest spoke in Arabic, and Corrigan turned to meet the rush of men from the car behind him and sprang towards them as they dashed forward out of the glare of the lights. He chuckled as he bounced his torch on the head of one man and pushed a big fist firmly into the face of another. Then the fight started in earnest. Corrigan couldn't count the number of them. They came rushing in from all sides and they went careering backwards when they ran up against his fists. He clawed one of them off his back and tossed him over the bales of raw cotton, and then suddenly the fight stopped and he saw that two of them, panting and heaving, were holding automatics which pointed at him.

' That isn't in the rules,' Corrigan said with a smile. ' We were just beginning to enjoy ourselves and now you've spoilt it.' He saw that there were seven of the Egyptians, all dark shifty men in cheap Western suits. Their greasy faces shone in the light. One of them was moaning, while another, with blood running from his nose, leaned over the cotton-bales and tried to be sick. One of the two Egyptians who were holding automatics had a little black moustache. His right eye was swollen and puffy.

Corrigan smiled again. ' See what happens when you play rough games ? ' he said.

The Purple Priest had been watching all this. Now he spoke again. ' You will be killed, Mr Corrigan. But not yet. I have a beautiful black cat which I show my guests. Soon you see it, but first you go through the door behind you.'

The two armed men led Corrigan through the door in the other side of the hall and down a long square passage cut out of the rock. It was dry and dusty, and the air in it was old and heavy with the smell of tombs. They came to another door which one of the Egyptians unlocked quietly. Corrigan walked through it and into a small square room which he guessed to be deep in the heart of the mountain. There was a candle in a bottle standing on a packing-case, and its still flame danced when the door slammed behind him. A trickle of molten wax slipped down the side of the bottle and blobbed on to the top of the case. There were two or three boxes on the floor, and a man was standing on the far side of the room and turning slowly towards the door. His lips were moving as he repeated something to himself and he was lost in thought, looking at Corrigan but not seeing him.

Corrigan recognised the crew-cut head and brown eyes of Geoff Oppenheimer. He grinned. ' Hello, Geoff. Expecting me ? '

Geoff was wearing glasses. He took them off and his eyes cleared as he came out of his dream. ' Corrigan ! ' he said. ' How in the world did *you* get here ? '

' I came with Shrimp. We came to see the sights.'

Geoff walked slowly forward. In the candle-light he looked paler and a little thinner in the face, but the old friendly smile was coming back. ' Say ! Am I glad to see you ! What brings you here, and where is Shrimp ? Tell me about it.'

They sat on boxes with the packing-case between them while Corrigan told him. He told him about finding Shrimp at the Pyramids, about Pappadikos and Hadrashi, about the bodies in the coffins, about how they found the tomb. ' And as I guessed,' he ended, ' it's all tied up with this Purple Priest character in some way. I'm hoping you can tell me more about him.'

' But where's Shrimp ? '

Corrigan leaned forward. ' He should be breaking all records back to Suez to bring up Pappadikos and his boys, if he's doing what I told him. Trouble is, you never know what Shrimp's going to do in a situation like this, but whatever it is, it usually turns out to be the best thing. Now tell me about yourself, Geoff, and the Purple Priest.'

Geoff shook his head. ' I can't tell you much. I was brought here in a car. They put a bag over my head and I'd no idea where I was going. All I know is that it took a long time, and it was still dark when we got here. I've been in this room ever since. I know it was Sunday evening when I was kidnapped, but I don't know how long I've been here.'

' It's Wednesday evening now,' Corrigan told him quietly.

Geoff's eyebrows went up. ' Wednesday ! You don't say ! I didn't know time had gone as quickly as that. So I haven't seen daylight for three days.'

Corrigan was looking puzzled. ' You say time's passed quickly ? How's that ? '

(1,824)

9

' I've been busy. Take a look at the walls of this room. There's a month's work here.'

Corrigan could see that the walls were covered with the painted figures of Ancient Egyptians and neat rows of beautiful hieroglyphs. He laughed. ' So that's it. You've been translating this lot.'

Geoff nodded enthusiastically and pointed to a thick note-book. ' That's full. It's fascinating ! It throws new light on the organisation of the Temple of Amun. When you came in I was working through a wonderful account of how Opi inspected the Temple workshops and gave orders for new hinge-posts for the Temple gates. I've got two or three weeks' work right here.'

Corrigan shook his head. ' So you've been quite happy ? '

' Sure.'

' And you haven't tried to break out ? '

' Not a chance.' Geoff turned towards the door. ' That's solid and it's locked. Not a chance, brother. I don't know why they brought me here, unless it was to stop me searching for the tomb, as you say. I've seen the Purple Priest only once. He's a fake.'

' How d'you mean ? '

' He isn't what he pretends to be—he's no Chief Priest. His dress is wrong in certain details.'

Corrigan chuckled. ' You surely didn't think that he was *the* Opi ? '

Geoff rubbed the top of his bristly head. ' I guess not. Although some queer things have happened in connection with these tombs. But he ought to have been dressed right. He had only to copy the carving on the wall in the entrance. I've seen him once since I arrived. He told me he wants a complete translation of all the hieroglyphs in the tomb.' He shook his head. ' I don't get it. What is he—a crook or an Egyptologist ? Only an Egyptologist would be interested in these hiero-glyphs.'

' If he's an Egyptologist he'd surely be able to translate them for himself.'

' It doesn't follow. There are Egyptologists who don't specialise in hieroglyphs. I do, and I guess he knew it. For some reason he wants a translation, but I can't think what use it's going to be to a crook.'

Corrigan sat thinking for some time. ' He may want to perfect his rôle as Opi, the Chief Priest,' he said at last, ' or he may be genuinely interested in the old boy, particularly as he's using his tomb as a headquarters. Whichever it is, it's been a good thing for you. If he hadn't found a use for you he would have killed you.'

Geoff looked startled. ' Killed me ! What on earth for ? '

' Because he wants nobody to know where this tomb is. He uses it.'

' What for ? '

' Search me. Selling raw cotton presumably.' Corrigan told Geoff about the bales in the hall. ' Seems an odd place for a cotton warehouse,' he went on, ' but there they were. And that reminds me of something else. When you saw the Priest did he have his cat with him ? '

Geoff's forehead wrinkled. ' Cat ? Which cat ? '

' It seems he has a cat,' Corrigan explained and smiled. ' He said he's going to introduce me to it before he kills me.'

Geoff shook his head. ' I haven't seen a cat,' he said slowly. Then he sat up. ' Wait ! Last night the men who bring my food were late—I get food morning and evening—and when I asked them why, they said they'd been watching the cat play with a mouse. That must be it, I guess.'

Corrigan nodded. ' Yes, and it's my bet that the " mouse " was the man who was delivered in a coffin at my hotel this morning. If I'm right this cat must be quite an animal.'

' Cats were very important in Ancient Egypt.'

' I think this one would be important anywhere.' Corrigan sat in thought for a time. Then he felt in his pocket and made sure his matches were still there. ' I'm trying to give myself a sporting chance,' he said to Geoff. ' You got any spare paper ? '

Geoff collected several screwed-up sheets of note-paper from the floor. ' There's this,' he said, smoothing them out on the packing-case. ' How much do you want to write ? '

Corrigan took the paper and pushed it into his pocket. ' I'm not writing anything. I want this for something else. You say you get food in the evening. Have you had it yet ? '

' No. I should think it's about due.'

'Right ! Two men bring it. Are they armed ? '

Geoff shook his head. 'No, they're quite friendly, in a villainous sort of way. They laugh and make jokes, or what passes for jokes with them. They speak a fair amount of English.'

'If they aren't armed the joke's going to be on them,' Corrigan was saying when the door opened. Two men entered. One carried a dish in one hand and a hunk of dark bread in the other. He placed these on the packing-case. The other man was carrying an automatic which he pointed at Corrigan. 'You come,' he grunted.

Corrigan glanced at Geoff. 'The joke's on me,' he said. 'I'll see you later.' He walked through the door, noticing how the Egyptians stood back out of reach, and into the passage. A circle of light from the torch of one of the guards lay around his feet as he walked the length of the passage and into the hall. He saw that the last of the daylight had gone from the ravine outside.

'You stop ! ' came a voice from behind him.

He stopped. One of these chaps is going to make a mistake, he said to himself. Somebody *must* make a mistake sooner or later, and when it comes I'll have to be ready for it. Maybe *I'll* be the one to make it. He smiled at the thought. The unarmed guard had gone forward and opened the door on the other side of the hall, and Corrigan now walked through this and along a passage exactly like the first. He went forward in the pool of light from a torch. At the end of the passage was an open door, and through this Corrigan came to a room similar to the one in which Geoff was imprisoned.

He stopped. Across the room the Purple Priest was standing, the Purple Priest with the candle-light flickering on his golden mask and helmet and two of his Egyptians on each side of him.

'Now, Mr Corrigan,' the Priest said in his soft caressing voice ; 'now, Mr Corrigan, you meet my cat.'

'Where's the milk ? ' Corrigan asked.

The glinting eyes flashed like black glass. 'There is no milk. I tell you about my cat. It is a big one, yes. It is unfriendly, yes. But my men, they like to have sport. So when we have a guest we introduce him to the cat. If the cat is friendly with him we are friendly also. If the cat is unfriendly '—he shrugged—' it does not matter. It is a custom we have here.'

'Sounds like a pleasant one,' Corrigan murmured.

'Not pleasant but wise, Mr Corrigan. In Ancient Egypt we appreciated the wisdom of cats and we respected them. Here we make use of that wisdom. Our cat decides if our guests are worthy.'

Along one wall of the room two of the ancient coffins were lying. Corrigan pointed to them. ' I was beginning to think you were a cotton merchant,' he said. ' I was wrong. You're an undertaker.' He was talking in a jocular way but his eyes were never still. He was waiting for the moment which must come, which always came ; the moment when his enemies were off guard. The light in the room came from two candles and Corrigan was shuffling imperceptibly nearer to the packing-case on which they were standing.

The Priest said nothing for a few moments, and when he spoke it was in Arabic and two of the men beside him immediately produced automatics which they pointed at Corrigan. ' This thing you say,' the Priest said in his softest voice, ' I do not understand. I do understand that you are thinking that you will knock over the candles, Mr Corrigan. This would not be wise. I read men's thoughts from their faces. Your lips smile but your eyes do not. They tell me that your brain works quickly and without fear. You have the eyes of a trapped lion, Mr Corrigan. Those coffins you point to we need. It is possible that we need one tonight.' He sniggered behind the mask. ' I mean if our cat does not like you.'

' You may need one for the cat if I don't like *it*,' Corrigan grunted.

' Turn round, Mr Corrigan,' the Priest ordered.

Corrigan turned. He was facing the door through which he had entered the room. Beside it was another door, closed, and in the wall at a height of about four feet were three long slits which he guessed to be for ventilation.

' You go through the door which is now closed,' the Priest was saying. ' Inside you find what you look for.'

' And what if I don't go ? '

Corrigan heard a metallic click.

' Then you are shot,' the Priest said.

The two Egyptians who had brought Corrigan were now standing one on each side of the closed door. One of them was the man with the black moustache and the puffy eye. As Corrigan approached he held the door ready.

Corrigan stopped. ' You have a black eye,' he said. ' You should look after that. Try a piece of pork on it.'

The Egyptian snarled at him and pushed open the door and Corrigan walked into a dark room. The door closed softly behind him and the darkness was complete and suffocating and heavy. He stood absolutely still. He didn't breathe. Very soon his eyes began to collect the little light which came into the room through the three ventilation slits in the wall. He heard a soft angry hiss and he made out a shape, blacker than the blackness, on the other side of the room. Quietly he took his matches from his pocket and struck one. The flame flared up and then burned steadily and Corrigan could see. He could see a black cat, a wicked angry black cat, the biggest he had ever seen. It was an Indian black panther. Corrigan began to sweat.

The panther's body was about three feet long. It was a moulded rounded concentration of silent power as it crouched, its tail swishing across the stone floor and its eyes flashing green hatred. Its ears and whiskers were lying back along its head as it slowly gathered itself for the spring.

Corrigan took the screwed-up paper from his pocket. It might burn for thirty seconds. He lit

The panther twisted and wriggled

one corner of it, watching the panther all the time but seeing the blue flame gain strength and turn to white, and then he tossed it gently across the room. He watched it with such intensity that he scarcely noticed the dying match scorching his finger. Everything depended on that little bundle of paper. It sailed through the air and its flame turned blue again with the coldness of the draught ; it dropped on to the stone floor, spluttered and coughed up smoke and sparks ; then it flared up in a joyous white flame and the panther, with a snarl, leapt high, twisted in the air and landed in padded silence with its back to Corrigan and facing the little bonfire. It was crouching, wriggling backwards and spitting.

In three silent strides Corrigan was behind it. In one smooth pounce he had seized it from behind, his big hands around its neck as he picked it up and held it at arms' length in front of him, with its back to him and its tearing claws and teeth slashing the air. He squeezed. The panther twisted and wriggled, coiled and snarled. He squeezed out the wickedness, the hatred, the cruelty, and still he squeezed. His arms were torturing him. The weight, the power and muscular anger of the big cat were being held captive by his two hands, and his arms were paying for it as his muscles bulged and trembled. But he kept on squeezing, and now the panther's struggles were weakening, now it had to rest, and now its snarls were choking gasps. Corrigan sweated. In that cool room, buried deep in the rock of a mountain, he sweated until he could feel it streaming down his face and chest and a trickle went along one straining shoulder and down his back. It tickled. The room was black, but there was a redness in front of Corrigan's eyes and a roaring in his ears and still he squeezed.

Then he realised that the panther hadn't moved for some time. It was lying in his hands, limp and helpless. He tried to straighten his fingers. At first they stuck, buried in the soft fur of the panther with their muscles paralysed, and then they untwisted themselves in a frenzy of pain, the panther dropped softly and Corrigan staggered back against the wall, sweating and heaving.

Gradually the torture in his arms died away, his heart settled down and the sweating stopped. He shivered. He wiped his face and pushed himself upright and moved his arms gently. He had gone cold and quiet with a fierce anger. In the darkness the panther gave a little sigh. The door opened, and Corrigan looked out at the warm candle-light and the Purple Priest standing on the far side of the well-lit room. He walked slowly out and stood in the doorway, filling it.

The Priest was with his six henchmen and they looked at Corrigan in silence. He could see fear, doubt and wonder go chasing across the faces of the six Egyptians, but the Priest's eyes, behind the slits in the gold, showed nothing.

' You killed it ! ' the Priest said at last. ' You have strength, Mr Corrigan.'

Corrigan nodded. ' I didn't want to kill it, but I had to. It's a filthy way to kill a man—to fasten him in there with that panther in the darkness while you watch and listen through those slits. How many men have you done it to? There aren't going to be any more.'

He moved towards the Priest slowly and the menace in his face, the deadly fury of his eyes held the Egyptians for a few moments. The Priest saw death and he whimpered softly and his six hench-men leapt at Corrigan. Corrigan struggled forward. His eyes were fixed on the Priest and he fought off the Egyptians like a man brushing off flies, until, when he was reaching out for the Priest and his hands were almost touching that golden mask, his vision splintered into shafts of light and he was falling. Darkness came.

Chapter IX

SHRIMP ALONE

It was growing darker in the ravine. Shrimp had been crouching on the rock-ledge for a long time, trying to make up his mind. He was still trying, when he heard a noise and looked up in time to see a big closed car come skidding and roaring along the bed of the ravine and swing into the entrance to the tomb. It stopped. For some seconds the noise of its engine went echoing away among the rocks, and then there came from the tomb a muffled shout.

Shrimp grabbed his rucksack and leapt down into the ravine and made for the tomb. He had almost reached the entrance when he heard Corrigan's calm voice. ' That isn't in the rules,' Corrigan was saying, and Shrimp stopped and stood still.

How many rules was *he* breaking ? Why wasn't he now on his way to the Packard ? Corrigan was relying on him, and all he had managed so far was a wasted half-hour of dilly-dallying. He turned and began to sprint in his light athletic way down the ravine.

When he reached the entrance he saw that the day was almost over. The cliffs and rock-faces of the Jebel had turned black and were pointing sharply up into the glowing sky, while the purple desert was closing in. Shrimp was blowing after

the run and he stopped to lean against a boulder.
He felt guilty. Out here he could breathe the free
desert air, like champagne in the evening, while
Corrigan had to breathe the mouldy air of the
tomb. But Corrigan had told him to go to Suez.

Shrimp looked south-westwards. It was that
clear time of the early night when all the dust and
heat are draining out of the atmosphere and leaving
it fresh and new. The lights of Suez were coming
up, coming out of the dying heat-haze, with electric
brightness. Shrimp snuggled back against the
warm rock and watched them, and gradually the
darkness became complete, the desert disappeared
and there was nothing but Shrimp and the lights.
Somewhere amongst that lot, he thought, would be
Pappadikos, little round Pappadikos with the moustache, munching salted sunflower-seeds and sipping
his aniseed. He would be sitting on the hotel roof,
and those brightly vivid eyes of his would be gazing
across the dark desert to Jebel Ataka.

Shrimp stood up suddenly. To Jebel Ataka !
He opened his rucksack and found his torch. His
hand was trembling slightly. Would it work ? He
pointed the torch towards Suez and began to tap
the switch. Slowly he tapped it out : ' Pappa,
your children need help. Pappa, your children
need help ' ; over and over again, until the strain
of concentrating on the morse made him sweat,
while the flash of the winking light stabbing the
message into the darkness made him dizzy. Would
it reach Suez ? Would Pappadikos see it ? Would
he understand it ?

The fresh breeze coming across the desert was cool and Shrimp moved back to the boulder and sat beside it. It was warm, the stone had saved some of the sun's heat and he began to feel drowsy. For a long time he nodded in a pleasant doze, from which occasionally he would rouse himself to gaze sleepily into the darkness. There was no moon yet and the stars were at their brightest, while the lights of distant Suez sparkled beneath a glowing haze. Shrimp stared towards the city until the lights played tricks and appeared to move. They would run together and then separate, come towards him and then recede. He was still watching through half-closed eyes, when two lights which seemed to be approaching and growing bigger refused to go back. He screwed up his eyes and tried to force the lights back into position, but still they came on. He sprang up, fully awake. The headlights of a car, like two staring eyes, were coming towards him across the desert, following the track over the pebbles. He saw them dip into a hollow.

Shrimp's heart thumped. This must be Pappadikos. Good old Pappa ! But was it ? Other people used that track. He dodged behind the boulder. The lights came on. At first they seemed only to move up and down and then they were lighting up the rocks around him, and a big car purred over the stones and entered the ravine without pausing. Shrimp scratched his head. *That* couldn't have been Pappadikos. The Greek wouldn't have known how to find the ravine.

Shrimp knew what to do now. He switched on

his torch and began to search among the pebbles.
They were mostly limestone, and he chose a long
thin one and went to a flat face of perpendicular
rock at the entrance of the ravine and began to
scratch. He worked slowly and carefully, making
the letters clear, and the effort pushed his tongue
out between his lips. Finally he grunted and
stepped back. In two-foot letters he had printed
the name ' Opi ' in such a position that anybody
looking for a sign must see it.

He realised suddenly that the rocks in front of
him were lighting up so that he could see his own
darkening shadow on them. He spun round.
Another car was coming across the desert, and the
beams from its lamps rose and fell like two great
arms making obeisance to the gods of the Jebel.
He dodged quickly behind the boulder, and when
he looked out again he saw that there were two
cars, the first very close and the second a mile away.
He knew that this wasn't Pappadikos. The lights
were too confident, too sure of their destination.

Shrimp waited. Very soon the first car came
up, its lights picking out the screaming word ' Opi ',
but the occupants missed it and the car went
straight into the ravine. Then the second car came
and Shrimp's heart waited for it to pass. It made
for the entrance and then, after a muffled shout
and with the crunch of pebbles, it stopped. Two
men got out and studied the scratches on the rock-
face. They began to talk excitedly, and three more
men tumbled out of the back seat and joined them.

Shrimp could see them quite clearly. They

were dressed in lounge suits and each man had a silk handkerchief tied over the lower part of his face. Excitement accelerated their unintelligible jabbering. In the darkness Shrimp crept out from behind the boulder and round to the rear of the car. He pushed his torch into his pocket and stood on the big fender of the car and crouched down, gripping the handle of the boot. Then he waited. Very soon the car began to shake as the men climbed back into it, the doors closed and, with a lurch which nearly broke Shrimp's arms, the car shot into the ravine.

They travelled quickly and for Shrimp it was pure torture. They swayed along the twisting ravine-bed and plunged over its roughnesses, and Shrimp's arm muscles ached and throbbed as each swing or jolt tried to tear him off. But he hung on and after a few endless minutes the car stopped. As the doors opened he heard voices, the quietly excited voices of nervous men.

He unscrewed his hands painfully from the handle and lowered his dead feet to the ground. Gradually the blood began to surge through his arms and legs and he stifled a groan. Then he looked along the car. In front of it the passengers were filing past a masked sentry who examined the card each showed to him, said something and turned to the next. The men he admitted walked into the light flowing from the tomb and disappeared into the entrance.

Shrimp had a coloured silk handkerchief. He whipped it from his pocket, tied it over his face, took out his torch and passport and ran forward as the last of the car's five passengers was going into the tomb. He held his passport out to the sentry. He was cool now and smiling behind the handkerchief. The tall sentry bent forward to look at the passport, and his grunt of suspicion died suddenly when Shrimp brought his torch down hard on the back of his head. There was the crunch of breaking glass, the sentry sighed, tottered for a second and fell forward on to the pebbles.

Shrimp opened the door of the car and looked at the instrument panel. The key-ring was still there and he took it, slipped round to the rear, unlocked the boot and opened it. It was roomy and empty. He seized the Egyptian by the shoulders, dragged him to the back of the car and heaved him into the boot where he lay on his side, curled up like a baby. Shrimp locked the boot and put the key-ring back into the ignition switch. He was panting.

He took a deep breath, adjusted the handkerchief over his face and walked to the tomb. The entrance was still blocked by a car but there was room for him to squeeze through. He was in the hall. It was lit by one electric bulb which hung from the roof and was connected to the battery of the car. It gave a faint light which was lost before it reached the farthest corners of the hall, but was enough to light up the three car-loads of men who had recently arrived. There were twenty of them, and they were kneeling on the floor in four neat rows facing the far end of the hall. There didn't appear to be anything for them to kneel to except an empty dais and, on the wall, the carving of an Ancient Egyptian with little men bowing to him. Shrimp whistled silently. The carving was something he could recognise : it was Opi, in golden helmet and long robe, but without a mask. Even in the poor light Shrimp could make out the proud and forbidding features of the Chief Priest.

He knelt at the end of the last row and waited with the others. Twenty-one of us, he said to himself, all masked, all kneeling, all waiting, and I'm the only one who doesn't know what we're waiting for. The stone floor was hard and rough and the position uncomfortable, and Shrimp began to fidget. The others, the twenty Egyptians, remained perfectly still and silent, except that, in the front row, one of them kept clearing his throat nervously.

Shrimp looked cautiously about. He saw the paintings on the walls, the door on each side of the carving and the bales of raw cotton. He was just thinking that they would be a lot more comfortable than the hard floor, when the door on the left of the dais opened and two men appeared. They were like all the others, dressed in lounge suits and masked, but each was carrying a large sack. They mounted the little dais and stood there, facing the kneeling men.

Then the waiting began again. Shrimp felt the tremor of nervousness which went round the Egyptians, and the man in the front row had an attack of coughing and throat-clearing. ' Suck a lozenge,' Shrimp said to himself, and grinned into his silk handkerchief. He tried shifting the position of his knees and almost groaned at the pain in them. Then he forgot his knees, forgot the rest of the men in the hall, forgot everything as he stared at the man who had just come through the door.

It was the Chief Priest, the same Opi Shrimp had seen at the Pyramids, and he was stepping on to the dais, his long purple robe sweeping the floor so that he appeared to be gliding. The light glowed on his golden helmet and mask, and when he turned to face them it shone from the golden disc on his breast. He stood between the two Egyptians on the dais and looked over the kneeling men. The glinting eyes behind the mask seemed to take them all in, strip the handkerchiefs from their faces and go past their faces into their minds.

Shrimp saw that the other Egyptians were bending forward with bowed heads and he did the same. He was glad to—so that those gold-rimmed eyes couldn't see into his. What is this? he asked himself. Is it a new religion or is it an old one reborn? Is this really Opi, or are these men mad?

The Priest spoke in that quiet booming voice and the kow-towing men straightened up. Then there was another pause while the Priest looked at them again before he spoke a few words in Arabic. At them a man who was kneeling in the front row, the throat-clearing nervous man, stood up and walked forward to the dais. He bowed low and then handed something to one of the Priest's henchmen, who took it and put it into his sack. The other henchman took from his sack another sack, very small and well filled, which he passed to the man at the dais, who bowed, retreated, bowed again and then turned and walked towards the entrance and out into the night.

Shrimp was so interested that he forgot his discomfort. He waited for the next move and it soon came. The Priest spoke again and another kneeling man stood up, walked forward and went through the same act, handing something over and receiving his little sack. But this time Shrimp managed to see what was handed over. It was a tight roll of notes. Money! So if this is some kind of religious service, Shrimp said to himself, that must be how they take the collection. But it appeared to Shrimp that the Egyptians were buying something, and paying heavily for it. He shook his head, wondering what was in the little sacks.

Then he jumped and gasped so loudly that the man kneeling beside him glanced at him. What was he going to do next? There was only one thing he could do. By now four or five of the kneeling men had gone through the silent process of bowing, buying and leaving. The first row of men had gone, indeed a car was just starting up in the ravine outside, and soon, too soon, only Shrimp would be left kneeling there on the rock floor of the hall, with the eyes of the Purple Priest spearing into him and the two henchmen smiling wickedly behind their masks.

Shrimp began suddenly to sweat. This was

tricky. This was one of those times when Corrigan should have been around. Once again the Priest had them separated instead of together. Should he make a dash for it—up suddenly from behind the pack, round the blind side of the car and away? He grinned uncomfortably and wondered how his cramped legs would work.

Before he could find out, two more men came through the door in the left-hand corner of the hall and marched slowly to the entrance and stopped. Shrimp glanced over his shoulder and saw that they were standing silently, facing up the hall, one on each side of the car.

That's that, he said to himself. Making a dash for it wouldn't get me anywhere. I'll have to try something else, something clever. What would Corrigan do in a spot like this?

The one thing Corrigan would have done would have been to stay cool and unflustered while that cold smile of his chilled everybody. Shrimp rubbed his damp face with the handkerchief which covered it. Then, quietly, he found his wallet, took out some notes and rolled them into a bundle and waited.

By now more than half the kneeling men had gone, each going to the dais when the Priest spoke and taking away with him a tight little sack. Shrimp felt cooler now. His sweating had stopped and he knew what he was going to do. He watched each man carefully. They all went through the same routine, with which they were obviously familiar, and Shrimp memorised every movement.

Now there were only four men still kneeling, one was at the dais and the second car was starting up outside.

Shrimp rocked from side to side on his knees to try to keep the blood flowing through his legs in case he should need them urgently. There were only three men left now. At the next call from the Priest the man beside Shrimp stood up and moved forward and took with him the sickly scent he was wearing. Shrimp drew in a deep breath of the cleaner air. Then there was only one man left and Shrimp saw him stand up, go forward, bow, hand over his money, receive his sack, walk back three paces, bow again and walk out of the tomb.

There was a long pause, longer than usual, while Shrimp's heart counted the seconds. Then the Priest spoke again in Arabic and he stood up and walked towards the dais. His legs were numb and his knees sore but he tried to walk steadily, not to run, and to appear casual and cool.

He reached the dais. The Priest was looking down at him, and it was impossible to tell from that golden face with its hooked golden nose, a dead face with live eyes, what he was thinking. Shrimp bowed and held out the roll of notes.

Nobody moved. Shrimp waited, holding out the money, but nobody took it, and slowly he lowered his arm to his side. A slight noise told him that the two Egyptians who had been guarding the entrance were now standing behind him.

Then a sound came from behind the golden mask. It was a soft hollow chuckle, a cackle of evil humourless laughter which grew louder and louder until it stopped suddenly, bitten off.

'We expect twenty guests tonight,' the Priest said, 'but we have twenty-one.'

The two men behind Shrimp came up, one on each side of him, and held his arms. One of them ripped the handkerchief from his face.

The Priest nodded, the mask and helmet rocking backwards and forwards like a mechanical doll. 'It is the other interfering Englishman,' he said, 'the little one.' He pointed to the wall and his voice rose to a scream. 'Shoot him!'

They heaved Shrimp over to the wall and stood him there, his back against the rock, alone. In front of him he could see the Priest, still on the dais, and the four Egyptians, all watching him through the slits in their masks and two of them facing him with automatics in their hands.

The Priest barked something in Arabic and slowly the automatics were raised. Shrimp watched them coming into line. He glanced from side to side. There was an open door and a dark passage on his left and the tomb entrance on his right. The ravine seemed a long way away and he had suddenly gone tired and weak. He sank down a little. The automatics were pointing right at him.

And then somebody spoke in a voice Shrimp knew. It was a deadly voice, filled with icy fury, but speaking in a calm matter-of-fact way.

'I wouldn't do that,' it said. 'Somebody might get hurt.'

Chapter X

THE PRIEST WINS

Corrigan came out of it slowly. First there was the headache, a thumping audible pain which burst inside his skull, but still the blackness. Then there was the lumpy discomfort of the rocky floor and the coldness of it against his back, and still the blackness. Then he opened his eyes.

He saw things at first hazily, like looking through unfocused binoculars, then more clearly, and finally, first the candle-flame, next the packing-case and then Geoff, sitting on a box and staring at him anxiously, came sharply into view. He tried to grin but his parched lips wouldn't stretch.

' I've sure been worried about you, Corrigan,' Geoff said quietly.

Corrigan sat up painfully and rubbed his face. I'm not too happy about myself either, he thought. ' Any water in that jug of yours ? ' he asked.

Geoff jumped up and brought the jug, his anxiety making him hurry. Corrigan drank. It was an earthenware jug, and the evaporation-cooled water was cold and clean and full of life. He drank slowly and deeply before he put the jug down on the floor and wiped his mouth. He shook his head tentatively and it seemed to rattle.

' Phew ! ' he gasped. ' How long have I been " out " ? '

' It must be two hours since they carried you in here and you were " out " then. They dropped you on the floor and I put my blanket down and lifted you on to it.' Geoff was wearing his glasses and he was goggling at Corrigan. ' It was some job,' he went on with a smile. ' You must turn the scale at two hundred pounds.'

Corrigan nodded. He was back in the prison-room again. Everything was the same except that he was sitting on Geoff's blanket. ' Anybody been to look at me ? ' he asked.

' Sure. The same two men were here not ten minutes since. One of them said they'd be back to see you made no noise. I've an idea there's something special on and they don't want you kicking the door in.' Geoff took off his glasses and put them away. ' You don't feel like telling me what happened ? '

' I'll tell you, but first we must be ready. I'm staying here on this blanket. When those two thugs come back I'll pretend to be unconscious. Then I'm going to have a crack at nobbling the pair of them. When the fun starts you close the door, and then, if you care to give a hand, it might speed things up a bit. Okay ? '

Geoff nodded and rubbed his head uncertainly. ' We're going to try to make a get-away ? '

Corrigan sat in thought for a few moments. ' Right ! ' he said at last. ' We're going to have a crack at it. But before we leave I'm hoping to collect that Priest so that we can take him along with us. I'll tell you about it.' He told Geoff about the other rooms and about the panther and how he had fought it, and how his rage had made him want to kill the Priest. ' Anybody who can put a man in a dark room with a thing like that panther isn't fit to live,' he went on. ' It's hard luck on the panther as well.'

Geoff sat and stared at him for some time in silence. ' That's it,' he said finally.

' That's what ? '

' The plan of this tomb. There's the entrance hall with two passages leading out of it. This room's at the end of one of them and there's another room, like this but larger, at the end of the other, and this other room has a smaller one opening out of it—the room where they keep the panther. Right ? '

Corrigan nodded and looked puzzled. ' Right. But where's the importance of all this ? '

Geoff was excited again. ' Well, this room where we are now must have been the burial chamber of Opi's wife. I was getting on to that from these inscriptions. They're full of how she was the light of his life and his constant companion. The other room would be Opi's burial chamber, and the smaller one—the panther room—that would be where they'd store the funerary furniture and his personal belongings.'

Corrigan stared at the American's face which was vivid with excitement, and then he laughed so hard that his head hurt. ' You'll be the death of me ! Here I'm telling you about the Purple Priest and his panther and all you can do is think about your Egyptology.'

Geoff was laughing with him. ' Okay, let's get back to the panther. You say you killed it ? '

Corrigan shook his head. ' I don't think so. I didn't particularly want to, except to save my own skin. No, I think I choked it until it became unconscious, and if I'd had to go on for another minute the panther would have won.'

There was a scraping noise outside the door and Corrigan lay back on the blanket and closed his eyes.

The door opened slowly and two men came into the room. They were the men who had come for Corrigan earlier in the evening. One of them, the one with the little moustache, was holding an automatic. He nodded towards Corrigan. ' He is not awake ? Yes ? '

Geoff shook his head. ' You must have hit him with something mighty heavy.'

The Egyptian chuckled. ' He has the hard head, that one.' He stepped forward. ' He sleeps like the baby—the very big baby.' He turned to his companion and said something in Arabic, and the other Egyptian walked to Corrigan and tapped him with his foot. Corrigan didn't move. The Egyptian prodded him again, and then bent down to look more closely at his face which was in shadow.

The movement was so quick that the Egyptian never saw it. All he knew was that his throat was held in a steel grip, a grip which choked him so that he could make no sound and which held him bent and helpless. He tried to squirm but it was too painful and he stood, still in that foolish, stooping position, slowly choking and looking down into the cold eyes of Corrigan who lay flat and held him with one hand.

The other Egyptian did not realise what was happening. He saw his companion bent over the Englishman in a constant stoop, as if his muscles had stuck. He called something in impatient Arabic and still the stooping-statue-of-a-fool didn't move. He cursed and walked towards him, calling on Allah to witness that the idiot must be the son of a paralytic cow. He was almost there when Corrigan's long legs flicked out, twisted round his and he was thrown backwards heavily. He lay for a second, gasping, then struggled to get up, but the other Egyptian came flying through the air and landed on top of him.

All this had happened so quickly that Geoff was still sitting on the box. Now he jumped up, ran to the door and closed it. When he turned round he was in time to see Corrigan pick up the two struggling Egyptians by their necks, one in each hand, knock their heads together and drop them unconscious to the floor.

Corrigan was grinning. ' That's better. I've given two headaches for one. Now we'll tie these jokers up.'

' What with ? ' Geoff asked.

Corrigan took the Egyptians' belts and fastened their ankles together. Then he tore two strips from the blanket and tied their hands behind their backs.

Finally he picked up the automatic from the floor and slipped the amunition-clip out of the butt. 'Ten rounds,' he said. 'This 'll be useful.' He made for the door. 'Come on, Geoff,' he said quietly. 'Let's go.'

With the door open, enough of the candle-light found its way down the passage for them to be able to see the far end of it. They walked quickly, Corrigan leading, until they came to the second door. Corrigan turned the handle gently and slowly began to open the door until he could see a crack of light coming from the hall. He pushed the door another fraction of an inch and peeped. He saw kneeling men, all masked, facing him, and a man standing at the dais receiving a small sack and bowing and leaving. He couldn't see who was on the dais. But I could guess it in one, he muttered.

Then he froze. His eye had been wandering steadily over the kneeling men and now he was looking at a man at the back, a man who interested him. His grin widened slowly. I've seen him before, he said to himself. A little pint-sized fellow with curly hair and a face like a shy angel ; a face half covered by one of my best silk handkerchiefs at the moment. Shrimp ! What on earth is *he* doing here ?

Corrigan signalled to Geoff to come and look and, with his mouth close to Geoff's ear, he whispered, 'Shrimp ! Disguised as an Egyptian. Don't ask me what he's up to.'

'What shall we do ? '

Corrigan chuckled. ' Nothing. Let the little perisher stew in his own juice for a bit.'

They watched as the Egyptians came, one at a time, up to the dais and left the hall, each with his little sack. They saw the two sentries appear and post themselves in the entrance : they saw the kneeling men come and go until there were only four left with Shrimp.

Corrigan chuckled again. ' Now he's beginning to wriggle,' he whispered. ' Maybe next time he'll do as he's told.'

Soon the last man was leaving and Shrimp looked lonely on the cold floor. They watched him get to his feet and walk stiffly up the hall and they saw him standing awkwardly there at the dais.

They heard the voice of the Purple Priest, speaking English this time. ' We expect twenty guests tonight,' he was saying, ' but we have twenty-one.'

In spite of the cruelty in the voice Corrigan's shoulders were shaking with silent laughter, and he nodded when the Priest continued : ' It is the other interfering Englishman, the little one.'

Then Corrigan's laughter stopped suddenly, switched off, and his eyes went cold.

' Shoot him ! ' the Priest had said.

Corrigan curled his finger round the trigger of the automatic, pushed open the door and stepped into the hall. ' I wouldn't do that,' he said. ' Somebody might get hurt.'

Everybody swung round at the sound of his voice and they all stood there for a second, staring.

The Priest looked like an ancient statue. Then one of the Egyptians cocked up his automatic but Corrigan sent a bullet whizzing off the rock between his feet, and before the explosion had finished thundering from one wall to another and out into the ravine the Priest and his henchmen had vanished through the door nearest to them.

Corrigan saw the danger to Shrimp who was standing beside the door. ' Here, boy ! ' he called. ' Over here ! '

Shrimp dashed across the hall, and the three of them dived for shelter behind the cotton-bales as the Egyptians began shooting from the doorway.

The concussion as one explosion chased another round the hall and rumbled off the solid rock of walls and roof was deafening. Geoff pushed his fingers into his ears and grinned ruefully. ' Funny games you two Limeys play ! ' he shouted.

Shrimp laughed. ' We're playing this one for *your* benefit, you lanky Yank,' he said. Then he noticed that Corrigan was looking at him. It's that queer look, he said to himself, the one that makes you feel quarter-size. He used to do it at school when you dropped a pass. ' I know what you're going to ask me,' he said.

Corrigan put a shot through the doorway where a venturesome Egyptian was showing too much of himself. ' Whenever you're ready,' he said quietly.

' I didn't like leaving you,' Shrimp grumbled. ' I thought of a way in which I could let Pappadikos know and still be here to give a hand.' He told them about the morse signals and the clearness of the dark night, and about how Pappadikos would be sitting on the roof of the hotel looking towards the Jebel. 'He must have seen it,' he ended. 'He'll be on his way now.'

Corrigan nodded slowly. 'He must be walking then. It's hours since you sent that signal. In fact the night's nearly over and he hasn't shown up yet.' He noticed the misery in Shrimp's face and he smiled. 'It's okay, boy. It was a good try. If it doesn't work we'll think up something else.'

'What 're we going to do *now*?' Geoff asked. 'Seems to me this is stalemate.'

Corrigan shot at a hand which was appearing out of the passage in which the Egyptians were sheltering, a hand which held an automatic. He missed, but the hand snapped back into the darkness. 'I'm going to have a go at getting to the entrance and out into the ravine,' he said.

'But if you go past the end of these bales you'll be in full view,' Shrimp objected. 'The Egyptians can see you but they're hidden down that passage.'

'Sure,' Corrigan nodded. 'But if I *can* reach the entrance I'll be able to shoot straight down the passage, and they'll pretty soon be ducking into the room at the other end of it. Then you two 'll be able to walk out in comfort.' He looked up at the ceiling. The bulb still hung from the middle of it and gave enough light to make anybody out in the open hall feel naked.

'First we'll switch that off,' Corrigan said. He

aimed at the bulb and fired. The splintering of
the glass was drowned in the automatic's explosion
and the darkness came with blinding suddenness.
' Here we go,' he whispered.

He crawled along between the bales and the
wall until he passed the last bale. Then he turned
towards the entrance, and already he could see a
lightening of the sky outside and he knew that the
dawn was near. He stood up quietly and was
about to step forward when he stopped, caught in
the beams of hard white light from two electric
torches in the passage. His leap and the double
explosion from two automatics came at the same
time. The Egyptians had expected him to spring
forward towards the entrance : instead he went
backwards behind the cotton-bales, and a little
starred hole in the windscreen of the car showed
where one of the bullets had gone wide.

' Not so good,' Corrigan grunted. ' We'll have
to think up something better than that.'

The two beams of light from the passage were
moving stiffly about the hall, flashing on the walls
and the entrance with the car in it, and some of
their light was thrown back so that to Corrigan
the faces of Shrimp and Geoff appeared like white
spirit-faces floating in the darkness.

' What are we going to try next ? ' Geoff
asked.

Before Corrigan could answer they heard the
voice of the Purple Priest coming to them from
behind the lights. ' You will surrender ? ' he was
saying. ' You cannot escape. You will surrender ? '

Shrimp gave a snort of disgust. ' Surrender ! '
he scoffed. ' We aren't trying to escape. We're
seeing to it that *you* don't.'

Corrigan grinned. ' That's the ticket,' he whispered. ' Let me come past you to the other end
of the bales. I'm going to try to get to the wall
and along it to the doorway. If I can reach it and
push my automatic round the corner, I can shoot
down the passage and then things are going to be
very interesting for the Priest and his boys. They
won't be able to see me.'

He crawled past the other two and reached the
end of the bales. In front of him was the passage
to the prison-room. He stood up and turned left
towards the dais and the doorway where the
Egyptians were sheltering. He stepped silently
forward and was stopped by a sound, a spitting,
hate-filled sound, and the panther bounded out
from behind the lights and into the hall. It stood
for a second, black and shining, its eyes glowing
green and its tail swishing in time with its anger.
Then it moved towards the bales and in one flowing
leap was on them, standing so near to Corrigan
that he could have touched it. It was lost and
confused, and the place was filled with man-smell
and cordite fumes which stung its nostrils. Corrigan stood very still, while Shrimp and Geoff
crouched behind the bales and looked up at the
black silhouette above them. Then, after an age
of silence and waiting, Geoff sneezed with all the
explosiveness of a held-back sneeze. The panther
leapt up straight, spitting, and then bounded

towards the fresher air it could smell in the entrance
and out into the ravine.

'Phew !' Geoff gasped.   'Sorry I had to let
that sneeze go.'

Shrimp smiled weakly.   'Sorry !   Why, you
scared the wits out of the thing.   The Priest's tried
everything now.   That was his last card.   He
hoped that animal would chase us out into the
open, but it didn't.   I couldn't have moved anyway.'

Four quick shots came stabbing out of the
blackness behind the torch-beams and thudded into
the packed raw-cotton, and Corrigan was suddenly
knocked sideways and the automatic went spinning
out of his hand.

He knew what had happened.   The two men
he and Geoff had left tied in the prison-room had
escaped and had rushed him out of the darkness as
he stood against the light.   He fought them silently
and in a few seconds had them powerless, with
Shrimp's help.

Then the torch-beams swung round on to them
and they heard the Priest again.

'You will all stand,' he was saying.   'If you do
not you are shot.'

Slowly they stood up facing the blinding light.
There was no escape.   Somewhere behind the lights,
where the darkness made a solid wall, the Egyptians
were standing pointing their automatics at them.

'You will walk through this doorway,' the Priest
said, ' and your hands you will clasp on your heads.'

They walked through the doorway and into the
passage, the way Corrigan had been before when

he went to meet the panther for the first time. There were now six of the Egyptians as well as the Purple Priest.

'Things don't look so good,' Shrimp muttered.

Corrigan had to stoop to prevent the backs of his hands scraping the roof of the passage. 'We'll think of something,' he said. 'Have you any ideas, Geoff?'

The American started. 'Ideas? I guess not. I was just thinking that I wanted to see this room and the inscriptions in it. It must have been Opi's burial chamber.'

Outside, the panther was padding swiftly down the ravine. It had almost reached the end of it and the level freedom of the desert when it stopped and sniffed the air suspiciously. Somewhere there were man-smells and man-noises. It swung round and streaked back until it reached the tomb again, a place it knew. The man-smell and the cordite-smell were still there. The frustrated anger boiled up inside it again, it snarled and leapt straight at the rocky wall of the ravine in one smooth liquid bound. It reached a narrow ledge and began to climb quickly, pouring up the broken rocks.

Just then the highest pinnacles of the Jebel turned light grey as the dawn-light touched them. They seemed to float against the blackness of the sky.

CHAPTER XI

THE FIGHT IN THE DARKNESS

As they walked through the door Corrigan caught Shrimp's whisper from behind him. ' Start something, Corrigan.'

He wondered what Shrimp was up to. He wondered also how you ' started something ' with your hands on your head while two thugs pointed automatics at your stomach. He sighed. ' If I see half a chance,' he said in a loud voice.

He walked into the room, followed by Geoff with Shrimp last, and stopped with his back to the wall. He remembered that the door to the panther-room was behind him. The Egyptians walked past him and stood in a line on the other side of the room, the Purple Priest coming last and walking in that silent floating way of his. He stopped among his henchmen. One of the Egyptians remained in the open doorway to the passage. So they stood in silence for some time in two irregular lines, captors facing captives, with a packing-case between them and on it a candle burning, its flame steadying after being disturbed by the movement in the little room. The two ancient coffins were still lying along one wall. The torches had been switched off and were now on the packing-case beside the candle.

Corrigan had taken all this in quickly. There

was only one chance and he wondered if it would come off. The candle-flame, smoking upwards, had given him the idea. ' What are we waiting for ? ' he asked.

Nobody answered for a few seconds and then the Priest spoke, his voice echoing round the room. ' You are impatient, Mr Corrigan. It is strange that a young man should be impatient to die.'

Corrigan smiled. ' You interest me. Who are you ? I've an idea but I'd like to be sure I'm right.' He was waiting—waiting for an easing of the tension, for a relaxation, for the Egyptian eyes to wander for a second.

' I am Opi,' the Priest was saying, ' Chief Priest of Amun-Ré.'

' You're a phoney,' Geoff grunted. ' Your dress is phoney and your talk's phoney.'

It seemed that behind his mask the Priest was smiling. ' Egyptologists can be wrong,' he said.

The eyes had wandered to Geoff, the tension had eased and Corrigan leapt sideways. ' Now, Shrimp ! ' he hissed.

It worked as he had planned it. An automatic crashed, a bullet went whining and spinning off the rock, the explosion thundered about the room and the candle was blasted out. There was a scuffle and a squeal in the doorway. Corrigan stalked silently forward into the blanket of darkness. He found an Egyptian and gripped his hot greasy neck, shook him and tore the mask from his face. Then he hit him and chuckled and went to find another, seeking the Priest.

There was a click, and a beam from an electric torch made a hole in the darkness, and a voice said, ' I shoot ! '

Somebody scratched a match on its box and the candle-flame quivered into life again. Corrigan looked around the room. Shrimp was missing, the man in the doorway was sitting on the floor and holding his stomach, and the unmasked Egyptian was fingering his swelling lips. He was the one with the black moustache and the puffy eye.

Corrigan grinned at him. ' Doesn't seem to be your lucky night, does it ? '

Geoff was still standing with his hands clasped on his head, and blinking at the candle-flame. He looked at Corrigan and smiled. ' You took me by surprise, I guess,' he said apologetically. ' I wasn't expecting anything. Next time I'll do better.'

' There will not be a next time,' the Priest said. ' You may put your hands down, Mr Oppenheimer.'

Geoff slowly lowered his arms and screwed up his face at the stiffness of them. ' I sure had forgotten they were there,' he said.

The Priest was looking at Corrigan, and his eyes, glinting in the darkness behind the mask, were like gems in the face of an idol. ' Several times, Mr Corrigan,' he said softly, ' you have surprised us. You are a big man but you move with great speed. It will not happen again.' He said something in Arabic, and one of the armed Egyptians stepped forward and stood about six feet in front of Corrigan with his automatic steady. ' I tell him to shoot you in the stomach, Mr Corrigan,' the

Priest went on, ' if you begin to move. To be shot in the stomach is very unpleasant.'

' I wouldn't shoot anybody if I were you,' Corrigan said. ' Shrimp's gone for the police.'

' He has a long journey,' the Priest replied. ' For police he must go to Suez and I think he does not get there. We have a sentry at the entrance.'

Not if I know it, Corrigan thought. Your sentry's miles away by this time, lying in the boot of a car. ' Sentries sometimes go to sleep,' he said aloud.

' Not if they are *my* sentries,' the Priest answered.

Geoff had been staring, his eyes screwed up in concentration, at the Priest. ' It's your head-dress that's wrong,' he now said, ' and your robe's probably the wrong colour.'

The Priest didn't take his eyes off Corrigan. ' I do not know if your interest in my dress is genuine or not, Mr Oppenheimer,' he said, ' but we are giving our attention to Mr Corrigan. Perhaps he would start to fight again.'

Corrigan grinned. ' You never know. Why don't you take the disguise off? It's years since I saw a priest of Ancient Egypt in the flesh.'

' There would be no harm. You will never have the opportunity to tell what you have seen, Mr Corrigan. You are going to be shot.'

Corrigan nodded. ' Sure. But let's have a peep before you shoot us.' He was talking—talking about anything. Seven pairs of dark and gloomy Egyptian eyes were watching him constantly, and he willed them to turn their indifferent gaze on

Geoff. Just for a second he prayed. 'What's the idea of the disguise?' he asked.

'It is necessary. As I use this tomb I dress to suit my surroundings. In my work it must be that the men who visit this tomb must not know me. I know them but none knows me.'

'Very clever!' Corrigan approved. 'And how did you manage to find this tomb which has been lost for years?'

'It was not lost, Mr Corrigan. It was found in the last century by a German, Dr Reisner. He tells nobody where it is except his greatest friend. His friend was my grandfather and he tells me.' Corrigan could hear the mockery in the Priest's voice. 'You could find out who I am from what I tell you—if you could escape.'

'Shall I guess?' Corrigan asked.

'It is not necessary,' the Priest answered. He turned and spoke in rapid throaty Arabic to one of his men who hurried out of the chamber. 'It is not necessary,' he went on, 'but it would be interesting to surprise you.'

'And what's the idea of this set-up?' Corrigan asked. 'What do you do here?' He was shuffling slowly forward, a millimetre at a time, towards the Egyptian who was standing guard in front of him.

'I guess he's a mortician,' Geoff suggested. 'He must be, otherwise why the coffins?'

'The coffins are for you and Mr Corrigan,' the Priest said. 'But I think Mr Corrigan will not fit inside one. The Ancient Egyptians were not so large.'

Then the Egyptian who had left the chamber returned, jabbering excitedly as he ran down the passage and into the room. The Priest listened to him and spoke quickly in Arabic, and then in English. 'You were right, Mr Corrigan,' he explained. 'Our sentry at the entrance has disappeared, and Mr Bradley too. This is a pity. We must hurry and for this I apologise, but we have not much time. It means that we must move quickly.'

'What are you going to do?' Geoff asked.

There was a pause, a silent throbbing wait, before the Priest answered. 'We shoot you. You first, Mr Oppenheimer. We take you into the hall and we shoot you. Then Mr Corrigan.'

I'm nearly there, Corrigan was saying to himself; another six inches and I'll try it. The chance *must* come when they start to take Geoff into the hall.

'We bring you back here,' the Priest was saying, 'and put you into the coffins and leave you in this room, where lay Opi, Chief Priest of Amun-Ré and Vizier of the North and South when Tuthmosis was King of Upper and Lower Egypt. You are to lie in Opi's eternal habitation for ever. It is to be yours.' His eyes were burning in the slits in the mask, and his voice was rising higher so that the rock rang with it. Then Corrigan struck.

He struck with tigerish speed and silence, his foot coming up in a long swing. It took the automatic out of the guard's hand and sent it clanging across the room, and before the guard's face could even show his surprise Corrigan had hit him. He went flailing backwards into the packing-case, at which Corrigan had aimed him, and he toppled it so that the torches went crashing to the floor and the candle-flame died. The darkness seemed as solid as the rock from which the room was cut. Only the little red spark on the wick of the candle glowed for a second or two before it died also.

Then panic was let loose in the room and Corrigan stalked freely about in it. An automatic spat fire into the darkness, and the explosion rolled around and split against the rock into a thousand explosions which grumbled as they died away. Corrigan was looking for the man with the automatic. Behind him he could hear the life gurgling out of the man who had been hit by the bullet intended for *him*. Then, as at a signal, the shouting stopped, the guttural Arabic oaths ended and there was silence. Corrigan stood still. He could hear the drip of blood on to stone, the breathing of men, the trembling of hearts. He could almost hear the Egyptians listening for him and he felt the waves of fear which came from them. He smiled. There was a man close to him, a greasy Egyptian who was shaking and sweating and Corrigan could smell him. He hit him silently and invisibly over the ear, and the man cannoned sideways across the room and the panic started again.

The automatic crashed a second time and the bullet screamed off the rock. In the flash Corrigan had a photographic glimpse of the Egyptians crouching about the room, of Geoff groping

forward like Blindman's Buff and of one Egyptian
opening a box of matches. The Egyptians also
caught a glimpse of him and three of them sprang
forward, cursing and grunting, and collided in the
spot where they had seen him. He wasn't there.
He was six feet away, knocking the matches out of
the Egyptian's hand and then hurling him into the
scrummage in the middle of the room.

He made for the man with the automatic.
Something was worrying Corrigan, nagging away
at the back of his mind, but he hadn't time to think
about it because the Egyptians had sorted themselves out and another breathless silence had begun.
He was standing beside the Egyptian with the
automatic.

The Egyptian didn't know it. He had his back
against the wall. It was cold and he was trembling,
and he wanted to squeeze the trigger and send all
the bullets boring into the blackness which was
smothering him. Then a hand clamped down on
the automatic which twisted with such force that
his breaking fingers had to let go and a steam-
hammer seemed to hit him on the back of the neck.
He went flying helplessly across the room, over the
packing-case and on to the rough floor.

The other Egyptians made for the sound. They
were learning the tricks of this blind fighting, and
this time they rushed silently towards the struggle
and found it. They found a man getting to his
feet. They knocked him over, seized his throat and
pushed a long knife into his heaving body. They
panted as they held him down until he was dead.

Across the room Corrigan was smiling and making for the rectangle of greyness which was the entrance to the passage. He went on past it until he found Geoff groping along the wall. He tapped him on the shoulder. Geoff turned quickly and swung a long fist at him, but Corrigan, expecting it, blocked it. ' Okay ! ' he hissed. ' This way ! '

He guided Geoff to the passage, pushed him into it and followed him, and in a second they were in the hall, bright with the daylight from outside. Old Opi still looked proudly down from the wall, the cotton-bales were in their place and the Egyptians' car still stood in the entrance.

Corrigan peeped round the corner back along the passage. There was light down there now. A darting torch-beam was seeking about. They'll find the other automatic, he said to himself, and they'll come with a rush. Then he remembered the thing that had worried him. In the flash from the gun-muzzle he had seen everything in the room —the Egyptians, Geoff, the packing-case, and that was all. There had been no sign of the Priest.

He made out a movement down the passage and he heard a soft scraping sound. Quietly he pushed his automatic round the corner and squeezed the trigger. There was a roar, a painful howl and a rush as the Egyptians scuttered back into the room. Corrigan grinned and looked for Geoff.

Geoff was starting the car. Quickly he backed it out of the tomb and then drove forward down the ravine and out of sight. He came running back into the hall a few seconds later. ' Blow out ! ' he

called. ' Bullet seems to have hit a tube. Can
you hold that gang in there while I change wheels ? '
He was breathing hard and his face was shining
with excitement.

Corrigan smiled at him and nodded. ' I'll have
a try.' The daylight was flooding into the hall now
that the car had been moved out of the entrance.
' Keep your eyes open,' Corrigan went on. ' The
last look I had around the room here, I couldn't
see anything of the Priest.'

' He was there when you knocked the light out.'

' I know. But he wasn't a couple of minutes
later. He might have been in the panther-room
but he *could* have got out in the excitement. So be
careful.'

Geoff nodded and rubbed the top of his head
thoughtfully. ' I'll be as quick as I can,' he said,
and turned to hurry out into the ravine.

For some time there had been no sound from
the room where the Egyptians were, nothing but a
deep and plotting silence. Now there came a
whisper and a bang—and a bullet went careering
off the passage wall and out into the ravine. Corrigan pushed his automatic round the corner and
fired. There was a pause and then another shot :
this time the bullet hit the open passage door and
screeched off into the hall. But Corrigan didn't
shoot again. He was looking at the long splintery
furrow where the bullet had hit the door in front
of him and he was thinking. ' Five shots fired out
of this automatic,' he said, speaking his thoughts.
' That means five left. They're trying to run me

out of ammo and I'll bet they have plenty.' He nodded thoughtfully. He guessed that there would be four of the Egyptians left in action, not counting the Priest ; four battered and desperate men. I'll have to be careful, he said to himself. I want to have a couple of rounds left when Geoff's ready with the car. Then I'll close the door, which ought to hold them for ten seconds, and run for it.

The Egyptians were busy. Corrigan could hear hammering and banging and the occasional grunt of Arabic. He wondered, and the silence which followed the noise worried him until he saw a shadowy movement down the passage. He peered into the gloom, trying to make out what was going on, and dodged back blinking at the flash of a gun. But he had seen enough. He had seen that the Egyptians had made a rough shield out of the packing-case and were now carrying it in front of them as they advanced slowly along the passage. Corrigan took a quick aim and fired. Over the roar of the explosion he heard the slap of the bullet into the wood and a grunt of satisfaction from beyond it. He fired again, this time aiming low at the feet on which the wood shuffled, and grinned at the howl of rage which followed the shot. There was a clatter as the shield fell and Corrigan heard the Egyptians stampede back to the room and safety.

He was beginning to worry. Three rounds left and still no sign from Geoff. He had another idea. He reached forward and closed the door to the passage. Then he leapt across the hall, seized one of the bales of raw cotton and dumped it heavily against the door. He heaved a second bale on top of it, and was about to return for the third when he heard a sound from the entrance and swung round.

He was in time to see Shrimp come dashing into the hall, followed by Colonel Hadrashi and a squad of efficient uniformed Egyptian police.

Chapter XII

THE EYE OF OPI

Corrigan was reminded of the rugger field, with
Shrimp, his cheeks glowing and his eyes shining,
jinking his quicksilver way round the other
team's pack. He grinned. 'You're soon back,
boy.'

Shrimp nodded. 'Yes. I met 'em half-way
down the ravine. Three cars, bulging with police
and the Colonel in the first one. They'd found the
sign I scratched at the entrance.'

Corrigan turned to Hadrashi. 'I'm glad you
made it, Colonel. Things were getting warm.' He
nodded towards the barricaded door. 'They're
behind that, the whole boiling of 'em, except the
Purple Priest. I'm not sure where he's gone.'

The Colonel's little eyes, set above the beaked
nose, looked very wise. 'Is good that we find you,
Mr Corrigan. We find this Priest later. What is
behind this door, please?'

Quickly Corrigan told him. He told him about
the fight in the darkness of Opi's chamber and how
he had missed the Priest. 'There's another room
in there, where they kept a black panther, but they
let it out. The Priest could be hiding in that room.
On the other hand he *could* have escaped.'

'You say six men are there?' the Colonel asked.

Corrigan nodded. 'But there should be only

four of them fit for action, and they'll be a bit the worse for wear.' He looked round the hall at the khaki-clad police who stood awaiting orders. ' I thought Pappadikos would have been here,' he commented.

The Colonel's eyes were almost closed as he looked into Corrigan's face. ' No,' he murmured at last. ' Is not at his hotel this morning.'

' But he had our message ? '

' Message ? What is this, please ? '

Corrigan told him about the message and the shop in Fuad Street. ' Only if we were in trouble,' he explained. ' If one of us was in difficulty the other had to dash into Suez with this message which was supposed to bring Pappadikos out at the double. Shrimp set off for Suez but flashed the message in morse from the end of the ravine, hoping that Pappadikos would see it.'

The Colonel was nodding, as he did when thinking quickly. ' So that is it,' he said after a few moments. ' Is clever that. We do not get Mr Bradley's message.'

Shrimp snorted in disgust. ' All that morse wasted on the desert air ! '

' Then how is it you came looking for us ? ' Corrigan asked, watching Hadrashi very carefully.

' Is simple, that. I know that you come to the Jebel yesterday. I know that you do not return. Today I look for you.'

Then Geoff came stooping through the entrance. There was a smudge of oil on his nose, and his hands were dirty. ' I fixed that wheel, Corrigan,' he said, ' and now it looks like we don't need the darned thing.'

Corrigan laughed. ' Somebody's going to need it. The four boys behind this door have to be taken back to Suez.'

The Colonel suddenly became brisk and decisive. ' Now we get them out,' he said. He spoke rapidly in Arabic, and the police removed the cotton-bales and put them along the wall. The Colonel walked over to them and began to examine one carefully, prodding it with a knife.

' You aren't thinking the Priest might be inside that, are you ? ' Shrimp asked.

For a few moments the Colonel didn't answer. Then he gave a satisfied grunt and lifted up a flap, like a trapdoor, in one side of the bale. ' Not the Priest, Mr Bradley,' he said, ' but what the Priest interests himself in.' His arm sank into the hollow interior of the bale and he drew out a bulging sack, sewn up at the end. He laid it on top of the bale and patted it lovingly and smiled. ' Now we see,' he murmured.

He started to cut the rough stitches carefully, one at a time, taking so long over it that Shrimp wanted to scream. At last the sack was open and the Colonel reached inside it and showed them a handful of light-brown shredded leaves and stems like dry coarse tobacco. ' *Hasheesh !* ' he said.

Corrigan nodded. ' So that's how they exported it inside bales of Egyptian cotton. And that's what those blokes came here for last night. They were buying *hasheesh*.'

The Colonel glanced up quickly. 'Who is buying, please?' he asked.

Corrigan told him about the twenty men who had knelt in the hall and had left, each taking with him a well-filled little sack.

Before he had finished the Colonel was nodding impatiently. 'We have these men, Mr Corrigan. We have police on the road and they stop the cars and search them. We find the *hasheesh* and we find '—his eyes were twinkling—'we find a man locked in the back of one of the cars. He has a lump on his head.'

Shrimp laughed shyly. 'That was the sentry. It was the only place I could think of where I could keep him quiet.'

The Colonel sat on one of the bales. 'These men are now in prison. I tell you. They buy *hasheesh* to sell in Egypt. You understand that my work is for a long time to catch the men who trade in this *hasheesh*.' He crumbled the dried stuff in his hand and let the powder fall to the floor, watching it as it trickled through his fingers. 'Is finished now, I think. We have them. The leader is this man you call the Purple Priest. This is something I do not know until recently. I have not heard of this Priest until Mr Bradley and Mr Oppenheimer meet him.' He smiled apologetically. 'You and your friends help me, Mr Corrigan. I make use of you and this is a thing I should not do. But '—he shrugged—' I try everything and I try this also. I think that you have the strength and courage and cleverness to do what my police, who are known to these criminals, cannot do. For this I thank you.' He stopped and his smile showed up the strain and the tiredness in his face. 'I watch you and I protect you as well as I can. I think you have enjoyed this also. Yes?'

'I've been on pleasanter picnics,' Shrimp said, but he was smiling.

Hadrashi stood up and slapped the dust out of his uniform. 'Now we finish. We have these men out of there, and their Priest.'

He walked back to the closed door to the passage and threw it open. The police took discreet cover. The Colonel stepped away from the door and called out in Arabic. He was answered by the crash of an automatic and a bullet plugged into the rock on the other side of the ravine. He shrugged and spoke to one of his men who brought him a small thick cylinder of black plastic. The Colonel took it, pulled a length of tape from one end of it and suddenly threw it down the passage. They heard the hollow plop as it landed.

'Now we persuade them,' Hadrashi said quietly, and took out his revolver. There was a moment's wait and then, from Opi's chamber, came an angry roar followed by howls of pain and an urgent scuffling and the four Egyptians came tumbling out of the passage. Their masks had gone and their eyes were streaming as they groped blindly about and cursed at the pain. In a second they were seized by the police, handcuffed and led out into the ravine.

The Colonel sat on a cotton-bale again and

they sat with him in a row watching the door to the passage. The police had left the hall and had taken the four criminals to the cars in the ravine, and the silence the tomb had held for centuries was beginning to creep back into it, a deep and brooding silence. The sickly-sweet spice-smell was still there, mixed with the cordite fumes.

' We have not brought out the Priest yet,' whispered the Colonel. ' We wait.'

They sat and waited in that hall which had been chiselled out of the solid rock some three thousand years ago. Geoff looked at the relief carving of Opi on the wall. Their wait was nothing compared with his, but he knew what he was waiting for. They didn't. His stony eyes looked down on them and Geoff saw pride and, perhaps, sorrow in them.

Corrigan was thinking about the last few days : about the night at the Pyramids, Pappadikos, Ahmed Badri, the fight in the Old City and about the Purple Priest. There's one thing certain, he said to himself. Whoever this Priest is, he knew every move we were going to make. As soon as he knew Geoff was looking for this tomb he grew interested in him, and then he switched his interest to us when he found that we were looking for it. We've found the tomb, but where is the Priest and *who* is he ? He glanced at Hadrashi. The Colonel was sitting perfectly still, watching the door, and his heavy revolver hung loose but ready from one hand. His profile, with the hooked nose and the deep slanting eyes, gave him a look of one of the painted two-dimensional figures of Ancient Egypt.

Shrimp was thinking that breakfast was late. His stomach rolled in revolt and he wondered how long this wait would last. He looked up at the carving of Opi, the priest with the pride and the scorn in his eyes. He started. Eyes! As he watched, one eye — the right — moved slightly. Shrimp stared. One eye was of rock, carved with all the cunning of the centuries : the other was a living liquid eye and it was looking at him.

'Don't look now,' he whispered, without moving his lips, ' but we're being watched ! '

Corrigan knew the tone of voice. ' What's up, Shrimp ? ' he asked.

Shrimp glanced at him. ' The carving !—Opi ! —somebody's watching us through his right eye ! '

Corrigan and Hadrashi swung round. The living eye had petrified and died. It was of cunning rock, like the left eye, but dead for all its cunning.

'Is an English joke this, Mr Bradley ? ' the Colonel asked in a cool voice.

Corrigan knew better. ' Tell us about it, boy,' he said.

Shrimp told them. ' I may be hungry,' he ended, ' but I'm not seeing things yet.' He smiled shyly. ' I tell you one of those eyes was real and it was watching us.'

Corrigan stood up. He picked up one of the cotton-bales easily and carried it to the dais below the carving. Standing on it he could reach the face of Opi and he pressed his thumb against the right eye. For a second nothing happened and then, like a cork plopping out of a bottle, the eye disappeared and left in its place a round black empty hole.

'It's a plug,' Corrigan said as he stepped down. 'I pushed it through and it dropped inside. There's a room behind this wall.'

'The panther-room, I guess,' Geoff suggested.

'Right!' Corrigan agreed. 'The panther-room it is. Somebody's inside there right now. He uses that false eye as a peep-hole. He's probably been watching us all the time. How about it, Colonel? Shall we go and get him?'

The Colonel studied his wrist-watch and shook his head. 'Is not possible, Mr Corrigan. The tear gas is too powerful. Soon—five, ten minutes —it is gone and we enter.'

'But it must be the Priest,' Shrimp argued. 'We have to get him.'

Hadrashi smiled. 'Cannot do, Mr Bradley. Patience! Without masks we cannot see him if we go in there. We are blind and he does as he wishes with us. We go very soon and, if Allah wills, we catch him. Now we wait. He cannot escape. Is impossible, that.'

'Unless there's another way out,' Shrimp suggested.

Corrigan looked at Geoff. 'How about it? You're the expert on tombs. Do they have back-doors?'

'I never heard of one, I guess. Not in this type of rock-cut tomb. They had enough work making one entrance.'

'There's something else,' Shrimp said. 'If that

tear gas is so powerful, how does *he* stand it ? ' and he nodded towards the inner rooms.

' He's in the panther-room,' Corrigan said thoughtfully. ' I expect the gas hasn't penetrated there.' He sat down again. ' I suppose we'll just have to wait.'

The Colonel nodded and smiled thinly as they settled down to wait. The seconds passed heavily. It was like the atmosphere of a dentist's waiting-room, and when the Colonel spoke again Geoff jumped.

' We go now,' Hadrashi said. He took a whistle from his pocket and blew on it ; the shrill noise rattled round the tomb. Two of the police officers came trotting into the hall, and the Colonel spoke to them quickly in Arabic and one of them handed him a big electric torch.

' We go in,' Hadrashi said to Corrigan. ' The other gentlemen wait. Yes ? '

' I'm not missing this,' Shrimp said in a level determined voice.

' I'm in on it too,' Geoff said.

The Colonel paused, smiled and then, with a shrug, walked towards the door to the passage. ' It is good,' he said. ' But there is danger perhaps. I go first ; you follow, please.'

They walked through the door and along the passage, the Colonel leading. Shrimp came last——his back felt naked and defenceless and the darkness was cold. Traces of the tear gas hung in the still air and stung their eyes. They came to Opi's chamber. The door was closed and the

Colonel stopped and pushed it slowly. It gave a hollow creak as he swung it wide. He held his torch in one hand and the revolver in the other as he led the way into the room. The room was filled with the smells of cordite, tear gas and death. It had become a tomb again.

The Colonel's torch-beam swung rigidly about and picked out the body of an Egyptian who was crumpled and lying in a pool of his own blood. The beam moved on, over the two coffins with their painted lids, across the remains of the broken packing-case, and then, with a yellow gleam, on to the body of the Purple Priest who lay on his back, stiff and straight, in one corner of the room. They walked silently towards him.

' So that's the end of the Purple Priest,' Shrimp murmured.

The Colonel stared at the robed figure. ' Is an unusual disguise, that one. Effective, yes ? '

' Wrong,' Geoff grunted. ' Those weren't the correct vestments of an Egyptian priest.'

Corrigan had squatted down beside the dead Priest. He wasn't satisfied. Something was wrong and he couldn't think what it was. He touched the tall golden helmet and it fell off the Priest's head. He picked it up and examined it. ' It's gold, all right,' he commented as he passed it up to the Colonel. ' Very thin beaten gold, lined with felt.'

' Take the mask off, Corrigan,' Shrimp said impatiently.

The mask was gold too. It was fastened by a

' I've seen this guy before '

179

strap round the back of the Priest's head. Corrigan
unfastened this gently and lifted off the mask and
they looked down on the face of the Priest. His
once-bright eyes were open and were now small
and dull, and he stared glassily through them at
the ceiling above him. His dead skin was dewed
over with moisture and his smart black moustache
looked out of place.

'I've seen this guy before some place,' Geoff
said quietly.

'I don't want to see him again,' Shrimp said.
There was something about the dead face which
was making him feel sick. 'Now he's dead I want
to go home.'

The Colonel's normally impassive face was working a little as surprise, disappointment and doubt
changed his expression. 'This man '—he pointed
—' *this* is your Priest ? '

'He's yours now,' Shrimp said, with a shudder.

Corrigan stood up, still holding the mask. 'He
isn't anybody's Priest,' he said quietly. 'You're
dead right, Geoff, you have seen him before. He
was one of the two men who came to the room
where we were locked up. I knocked them out
and tied them up. Remember ? '

Geoff's eyes lit up. 'Sure ! That's right, Corrigan. This was the guy who held the gun on us.'

It was dawning on Shrimp. Even in the reflected
torch-light he could recognise the confidence in
Corrigan's eyes. 'What 're you getting at, Corrigan ? ' he asked.

'I'm getting at the fact that this isn't the Priest.

He's one of the Priest's thugs dressed up in his robes.
I ought to have known immediately. There were
the Priest and six men—seven all told. We've got
four handcuffed outside and there are two here,
dead. Somebody's missing and I know who it is.'
Corrigan pointed to the dead man. ' I know this
chap. He has a black eye—I gave it to him. I
was never near enough to the Priest to give him
anything. I told this chap it wasn't his lucky night.
How right I was ! ' He looked at Hadrashi. ' You
aren't saying much, Colonel. What are you
thinking ? '

CHAPTER XIII

THE PRIEST GOES HOME

HADRASHI stood in silence for a few seconds and stared at the corpse.

'My thoughts, they are mixed up,' he said at last. 'Mr Bradley saw the eye of a man in the eye of a carving. Where is the man?' He pointed. 'Not this one. This one is dead. You say you have seen him before. I too know him: he is a bazaar-thief and pickpocket of Cairo. Often he is in prison but not for some time now. He cannot be the leader of these smugglers. He is not clever, this one—only cunning. Now he is dead. Who shot him?'

'He was shot while we were scrapping in the darkness,' Corrigan said. 'I told you about it. He was shot accidentally. The other chap over there was knifed—in mistake for me. It seems to me that we ought to be looking for the Priest. Let's try the panther-room.'

He led the way to the other door and opened it. The Colonel stepped forward.

'I first,' he said. 'I am police; you a civilian.'

They followed him into the panther-room. It was full of animal-smell, like a rabbit-hutch, which stung the nostrils unpleasantly. In the opposite wall a small round spot of light showed where the plug was missing from Opi's eye. The room was empty.

'Not here,' Corrigan murmured. 'He's escaped, unless there's another room somewhere.'

The white circle of light from the torch travelled slowly round the walls. They had the solidity of the rock from which the room was cut.

'Couldn't be that one of the four men we've caught is the Priest?' Shrimp asked, thinking aloud. He shook his head. 'No. We've only accounted for six and there should be seven. So where is he?'

'Could he have slunk away while the fight was going on?' Geoff asked.

Corrigan stroked his chain. 'It's possible. It was so dark that anything could have happened. That chap was shot right at the start of the scrap, so the Priest had something like four minutes to take off his robes, put them on the dead man and get out.' He shook his head doubtfully. 'Could be, but he'd need to be a quick mover. Besides, the eye . . .'

'Well, if that's what happened he's been gone for ages,' Shrimp said.

'We go now, please,' the Colonel grunted, and walked out of the room.

In a few seconds they were blinking in the bright daylight outside, and they walked towards where the cars were parked about thirty yards down the ravine. Corrigan was carrying the Priest's mask and helmet. He looked at his watch. It was nine o'clock and he realised that twenty-four hours ago he and Shrimp had just left Suez, and it was only sixteen hours since he entered the tomb. A pretty hectic sixteen hours, he said to himself, and I'm beginning to feel tired.

'I'm hungry,' Shrimp murmured.

They reached the cars and Corrigan put the helmet and mask on the bonnet of the first. Hadrashi had called his police officers together, and they were now standing in a tight semi-circle in front of him listening to the quiet brief orders he was giving. He paused once to ask Corrigan where Geoff's Packard had been left, and then he continued talking in Arabic. As soon as he finished, the four handcuffed Egyptians were bundled into the rear of their own car and two of the police climbed into the front and drove off down the ravine. Two more policemen followed in a police car.

Hadrashi turned to Corrigan. ' I send the prisoners to Suez,' he explained, ' and two of my men go to bring your car. Is possible that we need it. Now I divide my men into two squads. I take one up there '—he pointed up the ravine—' to search for this Priest. The other squad goes the other way, also to search. If we find nothing my men bring dogs from Suez and we try again. You stay here. Yes ? '

Corrigan nodded. ' Okay. We'll wait for you here.'

The two parties of police moved away briskly and a deep and stealthy silence filled the ravine. Corrigan squatted on the running-board of one of the two remaining police cars. The jagged pointed peaks and crags of the Jebel spiked upwards into the sky, a bright hard purple sky. Down in the shady ravine it was cool, but up on those baking rocks it would be cruelly hot. Corrigan could see that the walls of the ravine at this point went up about five hundred feet and that they were cracked and broken. The debris which had fallen from them lay in heaps on the floor of the ravine.

Shrimp had been exploring the rocks across the ravine, and now he came back carrying a rucksack and grinning hugely. 'We still have your rations,' he said. 'I left mine at the entrance last night. The jackals 'll have eaten those by now, but yours are all right.'

They ate cheese and biscuits, but their throats were dry and the biscuits stuck and went down uncomfortably.

'I'm dry,' Corrigan said.

Shrimp nodded and swallowed. 'Me too. Your bottle's over there in the rocks, but it's empty.'

'There's a jug in my room in the tomb,' Geoff said.

Corrigan smiled. 'Who's going to get it—in the dark, without a torch?'

Neither Geoff nor Shrimp volunteered, so they tried dates and then chocolate and these went down more easily. When they had finished Geoff stretched his thin length out on the gravel and yawned. 'I could sleep for a week,' he murmured.

Corrigan stood up. 'I think I'll stroll up the ravine,' he said, 'to see if the police have found anything.'

' I'll come with you,' Shrimp said. ' How about you, Geoff ? '

Geoff yawned again. ' Me, I'm staying right here.'

Corrigan and Shrimp set off up the ravine. Because there was now less need to concentrate on danger they could examine it more carefully. They passed the black mouth of the tomb and soon rounded a bend. There were odd plants of camel-thorn and of coarse stunted grass growing in the gravel and from cracks in the rock. Corrigan and Shrimp wandered on for about half a mile, passing a smaller ravine which came in from the left, until, ahead of them and in the distance, they could see the searching policemen swarming over the rocks.

' It looks as though they've drawn a blank,' Corrigan said. ' They'll have to get bloodhounds, by which time the Priest 'll be back in Cairo. Let's go back to Geoff.'

They turned and strolled back, and soon they came to the little ravine which joined the main one.

' Let's have a dekko up here,' Corrigan suggested.

The little ravine was only about twelve feet wide at ground level. There was a sharp bend to the right immediately after the entrance, and going round this they almost walked into a car. It was a small powerful Mercedes, maroon in colour and shining in its newness, except for the thin film of desert dust which had settled on it.

' Well, well ! ' Corrigan murmured. ' Now who would park a car here ? ' He lifted the bonnet and touched the radiator and the cylinder head. 'Cold,' he said. 'Or as cold as anything ever gets in this over-heated country.'

Shrimp was inspecting the instruments. 'Brand new! How long d'you think it's been here?'

'Dunno, Shrimp. All night or half an hour. It's difficult to say. The engine's slightly warm, but the sun's shining on the bonnet.'

'Then it could have been driven into here while we were up the ravine?'

Corrigan nodded thoughtfully. 'Possibly. But I should have thought that the police who went down the ravine would have stopped it.'

'If they were up in the rocks, which is where they probably would be, they might not have seen it. And sound does queer things down here, so they might not have heard it. Whose is it, Corrigan?'

Corrigan smiled. 'If it's only been here a short time, I wouldn't know, but if it's been here all night there's only one person it can belong to.'

Shrimp's face was glowing with excitement. 'The Priest?'

'Right! The police who went up the main ravine must have missed this one. Possibly they didn't begin their search so near the tomb. Or else they came in here and this car hadn't arrived.' Corrigan was beginning to feel uneasy. 'I don't like it. Let's get back to Geoff, shall we? It was a bit silly to leave him by himself.'

They hurried into the main ravine and down towards the tomb, and in a few minutes they walked round the last bend and saw the mouth of the tomb and, beyond it, Geoff sitting where they had left him stretched out, staring towards them. He waved urgently and they began to run.

Geoff had tried to sleep. His brain needed sleep but his body was uncomfortable, and it was a long time before he dozed off. Then the coldness of the stone beneath him and its unyielding lumpiness woke him, stiff, and he creaked into a sitting position, yawning, rubbing his eyes and conscious of the wrongness of something. He had been dreaming one of those hard dreams of daylight sleep, when the thoughts of consciousness merge grotesquely into the fantasy of unconsciousness. In his dream he had seen himself stretched on the gravel in sleep, while creeping towards him was the gilded Priest. He shuddered and looked towards the empty blackness of the tomb. No Priest. He yawned and rubbed his face briskly, and then his mind jerked him into full wakefulness and he swung round again. He was right. In the black shadow inside the tomb there was something lighter, some-thing which was moving stealthily, coming out. Then he saw Corrigan and Shrimp come swinging down the ravine and relief flooded over him, warming him. He waved.

They came dashing over the gravel, Shrimp for all his smallness running with twinkling speed and keeping pace with Corrigan's great long-striding burst. Geoff climbed to his feet as they came up. He pointed. ' In there ! ' he gasped. ' There's somebody in the tomb ! '

Corrigan and Shrimp swung round. They saw the dim figure in the black rectangle of the tomb entrance, a man who appeared to be watching them. Corrigan's face set in the way Shrimp knew so well, the firm mouth and the chilly ice-blue eyes.

' What 're we going to do ? ' Shrimp asked.

' I'm going in there to get him,' Corrigan said in a cold even voice.

He started forward in a lazy-looking walk which kept Shrimp and Geoff striding out to stay with him. The figure swayed, receded and then came back again. There was no recognisable detail. It was just a man-shaped blur of lighter darkness, where the figure caught some of the light from outside and saved it from dying in the depths of the tomb.

Now they were twenty yards away and Geoff was sweating. Fifteen yards away and the figure moved again ; ten yards—and out of the tomb a man stepped, a round, fat and powerful man with two little glinting eyes almost buried in the flesh of his face, and a big moustache. They stopped.

' It's Pappadikos ! ' Shrimp said with a laugh. ' I knew you'd come, Pappa, but you left it late.'

The Greek came up to them, smiling. His face was shining with sweat and he wiped it with a silk handkerchief. ' Bah ! It is hot ! I find you—the big Engleeshman and his friend.' He looked up at Geoff. ' You are the American who cause this trouble ? '

' Sure ! ' Geoff nodded, and then looked startled. ' What trouble ? '

Pappadikos shrugged. ' All Egypt looks for you, my friend, and Pappa finds you. You are an Egyptologist ? '

' Yeah—of a sort.'

' Then your stay in Opi's Tomb has not been wasted. You have been reading the writings on the walls to pass your time ? It is good. Now we go back to Suez ? '

' Not yet,' Corrigan said softly. ' There's something to be done first.'

Pappadikos pursed his lips. ' First ? What is it that we do ? '

' Find the Priest.'

' Priest ? You make joke, my big friend. Is not our Colonel here with his police ? He will find this Priest for you.'

' I don't think so,' Corrigan persisted. ' I think *we'll* find him. Come to the cars. I've something to show you.'

As they went back Shrimp walked beside Pappadikos. He was genuinely pleased to see the Greek and he was thinking that Corrigan looked sour and unnecessarily serious. ' You had our message, Pappa ? ' he asked.

For a second Pappadikos was startled. ' Message ? How is this ? You go to Fuad Street ? '

Shrimp shook his head. ' No, I flashed the message with my torch.'

The Greek nodded thoughtfully. ' You signalled ? This I did not see, but it is clever. Yesterday I had many things to do.'

' But how did you know that we needed help ? '

' This I am sure about. It is easy. You go and you do not come back, so—pouff ! '—he blew out his cheeks and let the air go with an explosion— ' here is Pappa ! '

Corrigan glanced over his shoulder. ' But you knew that we expected to be away for three days.'

' Yes, yes. But also I knew that others come to the Jebel last night—men who are dangerous. Oh, Pappa knows these things, so he comes this morning to see if you need help.'

' Is that your car, the Mercedes up the ravine ? ' Shrimp asked.

' Car ? Auto ? But yes. I hide it there where it will not be seen because everybody is missing and I do not know what is happening.'

' I was asleep on the gravel,' Geoff said. ' You must have driven right past me.'

Pappadikos shook his head. ' I do not see you. I see nobody.'

They reached the police cars and Corrigan picked up the golden mask and helmet. He handed them to Pappadikos. ' Ever seen these before ? ' he asked.

The Greek took them and examined them. ' Gold ! ' he murmured. ' Gold, yes. But not heavy. Where you find these ? '

' They weren't lost,' Corrigan said softly. ' You left them behind.'

It took a few seconds for this to sink into Shrimp's mind, and when it did he stepped back quickly. Crazy ! he said to himself. Crazy ! But Corrigan's always dead sure before he comes out with a thing like this. Geoff was rubbing his head and trying to make sense of it all.

'Again, please,' Pappadikos was saying.

Corrigan smiled. 'I said you left them behind. Why don't you put them on? We know you better that way.' He was still smiling with his lips.

But it was Corrigan's eyes that Pappadikos was watching; cold merciless eyes which stared straight into his mind. He shivered. Then sudden anger flared up inside the little Greek, his expression changed, and in the working of his face they could see hate, greed and evil.

He snarled some Arabic curse, dropped the mask and helmet and, without warning, sprang back and ran for the nearest wall of the ravine. Before they could stop him he had reached the rocks, and with unexpected podgy agility he leapt at them. Desperation drove him up the side of the ravine like a fat old monkey, and Corrigan went after him, climbing with long-legged ease. When Corrigan was about twenty feet up the rock-face he heard a commotion below and looked down to see Colonel Hadrashi come sprinting down the ravine, his face streaming with sweat. He saw the Colonel level his heavy revolver at Pappadikos.

'Hold it!' Corrigan called. 'Let's get him alive.'

'I shoot,' Hadrashi grunted. 'You come down, please.'

'Well, wait till I get down,' Corrigan said, and quickly climbed back to the bed of the ravine. 'Let's catch him, Colonel,' he went on. 'You don't want to shoot him now.'

'Don't people get a trial in this country?' Geoff growled.

Hadrashi's eyes glinted angrily. 'This man is wicked. He kills without trial; he dies without trial. For some time I know he leads this gang but I cannot prove it. Now I catch him.'

'You're too late,' Corrigan said quietly. 'He's caught himself.'

They looked up. Pappadikos was fifty feet above them. He had reached a narrow ledge which curved gently upwards and disappeared into a wide cleft in the rock-face. Out of this cleft had stepped the black panther, silent, trapped and menacing. Ten feet from him on another ledge it faced Pappadikos, and its tail twitched angrily and its little ears lay back along its head. It snarled. They could see the damp whiteness of the Greek's face and the sweat which had broken from his skin. He looked old, and his lips moved uncertainly as he tried to speak to the panther which was slowly settling into a crouch.

The panther was trapped, lost in a hateful waterless world, defiant and filled with animal spite. It sprang. Its leap was a flowing thing of grace and beauty; a wicked frightening thing full of claws and fangs and black fur rippling over muscle, and as it left the ledge the Colonel's revolver sent a crash echoing away amongst the peaks of the Jebel and a bullet bursting into the panther's little brain. It was a proudly defiant animal which leapt: it was a dead bundle of bone, muscle and fur which hurtled into Pappadikos and brought

It sprang

him with it off the ledge. They toppled together and crumpled together into the gravel on the bed of the ravine, and Pappadikos lay twisted, with the head of the dead panther on his chest.

Corrigan reached them first. He pulled the animal away and went down on his knees beside the man. 'He's alive,' he said to the others.

Pappadikos opened his eyes, those bright little eyes which now seemed brighter than ever. He said something in a language they didn't know. Then he smiled. 'The big Engleeshman,' he whispered. 'You win. I said that the Engleesh never buy from Pappa. They want something for nothing. You have my life.' He closed his eyes and when he opened them again they were going dull. 'Where is this Colonel?' he asked in a faint voice. 'This Hadrashi of the police who cannot catch Pappa?'

Again his eyes closed and he was very still so that they thought him dead. Suddenly he struggled to sit up and his eyes fluttered open, filmy by now and seeing nothing. 'I am Opi, Chief Priest of Amun-Ré!' he said in a loud voice. 'I go to my eternal habitation!'

His body went rigid and then collapsed, and he sank back on the gravel and stared upwards through his dead eyes. He was smiling.

Chapter XIV

THE COLONEL EXPLAINS

CORRIGAN stood up slowly. The silence was so
heavy that he felt he would have to push it away.
He looked at Hadrashi. 'You knew he was the
Purple Priest?'

The Colonel nodded. 'Yes. Is some time now
that I know he leads these smugglers. But I have
not the proof of this. You understand?' He
shrugged. 'Now—*mafeesh*! Is finished.'

Geoff was rubbing his head and looking mourn-
fully down at Pappadikos. 'Looks queer, doesn't
he? I feel kinda sorry for him.'

'Sorry!' Shrimp blurted out. 'Why, he was
going to kill you.'

'He killed many,' Hadrashi said. 'This man
even kills his own brother, who works for our
Security Services.'

'Why did he do that?' Corrigan asked.

'Is probable that his brother has found the
truth. So he must die. Now this one too is dead.'
Hadrashi looked at Corrigan. 'Where is it you
find Pappadikos, please?'

Corrigan told him how Pappadikos had come
out of the tomb and how he had shown him the
golden mask and helmet.

The Colonel was nodding rapidly. 'You knew

that Pappadikos was this Priest? How is this, please?'

Corrigan grinned down at him. '*You* knew, didn't you? You tell me.'

'For me this is easy. I put—how is it?—two and two together. Yes? This Pappadikos knew everybody, he has the chance to do this, he is the trader.' The Colonel shrugged. 'I guess it.'

Corrigan was still grinning. 'Me too. I guessed. There didn't seem to be anybody else it could be. And he made one slip—a little one, but it helped. He suggested that Geoff had been reading the hieroglyphs in the tomb. Now the only people who could know that are those who were in the tomb with Geoff. Therefore Pappadikos was in the tomb, and, as we hadn't seen him, he must have been disguised. Therefore he was the Priest. *QED*.'

'Say, that's dead right,' Geoff said. 'He did say I'd been reading the hieroglyphs. But he could have guessed it.'

Corrigan nodded. 'I know, but there were other things as well. The fact of his being here at all, and coming out of the tomb, was fishy. He'd arrived and parked his car without anybody seeing him.'

'His car?' the Colonel queried. 'What is this, please?'

'We found it,' Shrimp explained, and told the Colonel where the Mercedes was hidden. 'There's something else that bothers me,' he went on. 'We searched the tomb and found no Pappadikos.

Where was he? He certainly came out of the tomb just now.'

Hadrashi smiled. 'Is only one place where Pappadikos hides and we do not seek.' He gave Corrigan a sly look. 'Is my fault that we do not look in this place, as matter of fact. You know it, Mr Corrigan?'

'Sure. But actually there are *two* places where he could have been hiding.'

'The coffins!' Shrimp burst out, and his eyes were shining with sudden understanding. 'We never looked inside them.'

'Right!' Corrigan agreed. 'The coffins it was. And inside one of them he wouldn't be affected by the tear gas so easily. I think he must have hidden there while we were fighting in the darkness, and then, after his four thugs had left, he climbed out and made a dash for the panther-room, another place the tear gas wouldn't reach.'

The Colonel was nodding again. 'Is correct. I ask the four prisoners where the Priest is before I send them to Suez and they say he has vanished.'

Corrigan was thinking about Pappadikos squeezed into the ancient coffin, breathing the little scented air inside it and listening in the blackness to the sounds of their voices as they searched the tomb. 'He was clever,' he said quietly; 'clever and quick. After I pushed the plug out of the carving of Opi he must have gone back into the coffin to wait for us. Then, when he thought the coast was clear, he came out.'

They stood and looked down at the body of the

fat Greek. He was still smiling, and his face was now white and shining with a dead waxiness. A bright fly was running excitedly across his forehead. Beside him the panther lay, its mouth open and its tongue heaped loosely on the gravel.

Shrimp shuddered. ' I vote we go,' he said.

The police were returning, and at the same time Geoff's Packard came roaring up the ravine.

' Is finished,' Hadrashi said. ' We go now.' He turned to his men who were grouping themselves about, watching with indifferent curiosity, and spoke to them in Arabic. Then he looked at Corrigan. ' You go in your auto, please. I follow. I come to your hotel in Suez.'

' Make it soon,' Corrigan said. ' There are several things I want to know.'

The dining-room of the Hotel Splendide was small and homely. It was early afternoon and Corrigan, Shrimp, Geoff and the Colonel were having lunch. A hot shower had dissolved their tiredness and now, in fresh clean clothes, and eating a good meal, they felt bright and alert. Geoff was thinking about the tomb with its unread hieroglyphs, like somebody looking forward to finishing a good book. Shrimp was wondering whether they could catch tomorrow's plane for England, and hoping that the English air still had its biting freshness. He was tired of hot places ; places with a Turkish-bath atmosphere.

Corrigan was thinking about Pappadikos and fitting the odd unexplained bits of the story into place. He was trying to understand the Greek's character. A man who murdered for greed; a man who killed his brother for safety. A man who liked mystery, dressed up for mystery, created mystery; a cotton-merchant, a dealer in antiques, a trader in wild animals. All these added up to a fat little Greek with a big moustache. 'A strange character,' Corrigan said thoughtfully, 'but a fascinating one.'

Shrimp jerked himself back to the present. 'Who?' he asked.

'Pappadikos.' Corrigan looked at Hadrashi. 'Colonel, there are one or two things I don't understand. Who, for instance, burgled our room in Cairo?'

'Is easy, that one. You remember the big Sudanese, the hall-porter and commissionaire?' Corrigan nodded and Hadrashi continued: 'Is the burglar. As matter of fact Pappadikos persuaded Ahmed Badri to give work to the Sudanese. He must have somebody at the Oasis Hotel he can trust. He knows about Badri's interest in the tomb.'

Shrimp chuckled. 'I don't mind admitting that I thought Badri was the Purple Priest. He seemed cut out to play the villain.'

'He always appeared okay to me,' Geoff said.

'It is Pappadikos who is the criminal,' Hadrashi went on. 'He has great powers, that one. Now it destroys him. This Sudanese burgles your room and puts you to sleep with chloroform, and the next day, after you have left, he puts Mr Oppenheimer's camera into your room and then " finds " it. Ahmed Badri is an honest man. He comes to

Suez, where he has another hotel, so he brings the camera to you. The Sudanese has put the message from Pappadikos into the case.'

' So you'll be arresting him, will you ? ' Shrimp asked.

The Colonel nodded. ' Is done—after I return to Suez this morning. It was this Sudanese who telephones Pappadikos to tell him that you go to the Pyramids at night. He knows already, does Pappadikos, that Mr Oppenheimer is in Egypt to find the Tomb of Opi, so he thinks this is the chance to kidnap him and also to get rid of his brother's body, which he does not want. He hopes also to frighten Mr Corrigan and Mr Bradley.' He smiled. ' But you do not frighten very easily.'

' Don't we ? ' Shrimp said. ' There were times when I was scared stiff.'

Corrigan grinned at him. ' In future you'll maybe do what you're told to do instead of getting some crack-brained notion of your own.'

' Crack-brained ! ' Shrimp gasped. ' Why, it was brilliant ! ' He had a sudden thought and turned to the Colonel. ' What would have happened if I'd done as Pappadikos suggested ? If I'd called at the shop down the street and told old Methuselah that we needed help ? '

' Is not Methuselah, that one,' the Colonel answered without a smile. ' Is Ahmed Abassi as matter of fact. He smokes *hasheesh*. If you went to him for help you would be taken to the room behind the shop and there a man with a knife is waiting for you. He stabs you—so ! ' Hadrashi brought his hand down on the table in a stabbing movement. ' Your body is taken out at night and dropped into the Red Sea. Many sharks in the Red Sea. But this will not happen now. Abassi is arrested also.'

Shrimp shuddered. ' Sounds as if my idea wasn't so bad after all.'

' Is good that you do not come to Ahmed Abassi for help. He is a man of Pappadikos.' He leaned on the table. ' I tell you. Pappadikos fears to kill you in Cairo. He sees that you will not go to England until you find Mr Oppenheimer, so he must get you to Suez, where is better chance for murder. He tries to kill Mr Corrigan in Cairo, in the Old City. Is failure that because Mr Corrigan is too strong for these bazaar-thieves and *hasheesh*-smokers, and I watch and follow him.'

' Yes, but *you* sent us to Pappadikos in the first place,' Corrigan interrupted.

Hadrashi was nodding again and his smile was doubtful and apologetic. ' Is true, that. For this I have said I am sorry. Now it is finished, my stomach is aching at the danger. I send you. I think Pappadikos is the chief of the *hasheesh* smugglers, but I have no proof and I cannot get proof. So—I use you.' He spread his hands and smiled again, and his little eyes were twinkling with humour. ' I see that you are not easily made afraid and that you intend to find Mr Oppenheimer. I am a desperate man. Too long I have tried and too long I have failed. I must do something to Pappadikos to—to——'

' To force his hand ? ' Shrimp suggested.

' Is good that ! To force his hands. Yes. So I send you. He must get you to Suez and then to Jebel Ataka where murder is easy. He cannot tell you anything when you, Mr Corrigan, visit his shop, because Badri is there also, so he sends you the message on papyrus and tells you to destroy it. He does not wish that the message is seen by me because it is the clue which leads to him, so the Sudanese burgles your room and chloroforms you to be sure you have not kept the papyrus—that you have destroyed it. He does not know that I am there and that you show me the message. The next day you go to Suez. He goes too and I also. In Suez he arranges that you go to Jebel Ataka, and, in case one of you escapes, he arranges that you come to this shop in Fuad Street where you can be killed.' Hadrashi smiled. ' Is all, that. Now—*mafeesh* ! '

' Not quite,' Corrigan said. ' What about Abdul the Lame ? Why did Pappadikos send his body to us ? '

' Why he kills him is easy. Is because you have seen him and you will recognise him. I am not sure why he sends Abdul's body to you. I think it was not to make you afraid—that he has tried several times—but to make you angry. Then you will not forget to go to the Jebel.'

' To make us more determined than ever,' Corrigan said thoughtfully. ' He succeeded, too. What about the manager of this hotel—Alphonse ? '

' Is on the side of the police. He helps us. He

tells me about your talk with Pappadikos on the roof of the hotel and about the body of Abdul.'

'So that's that!' Shrimp said. 'The end of the case of the Purple Priest! Now can we go home?'

Hadrashi smiled. 'Is an aeroplane to England from Almaza tomorrow morning.'

'Well, we'll be aboard it,' Shrimp said, 'if we can get there.'

'I'll run you into Cairo,' Geoff volunteered, 'and see you off.'

'Is something I would like to do, this,' Hadrashi said firmly. 'Mr Corrigan and Mr Bradley have helped me much.'

'Sure.' Geoff nodded. 'They haven't done so badly for me either, I guess. So if it's okay with you *I'll* be taking them to the airport.'

Corrigan laughed. 'You can both take us. Shrimp 'll travel with one of you and I'll go with the other.'

Alphonse came tripping across the dining-room, rubbing his hands. '*M'sieur* Badri waits in the lounge. He sends his salutations and hopes that he may meet you, *messieurs*.'

'Let's hope he hasn't found another camera,' Corrigan murmured, and then to the manager: 'Tell him we'll be there in a few minutes.' He watched the Frenchman skip daintily out of the room and then he turned to Hadrashi. 'I think we'd better be nice to friend Badri. We owe it to him after all the nasty suspicion we had of him. I wonder what he wants?'

'Is easy this.' The Colonel was smiling. 'Badri has hotels in Cairo and Suez. This is his business. But his love is Ancient Egypt. For long he is interested in the Tomb of Opi. As matter of fact, once—many years ago—he tries to find it. He has a theory—yes?—that Opi is his ancestor. Now Pappadikos knew of this and he told Badri that he could get for him a translation of the inscriptions in the tomb, but he would not tell him where the tomb is. Badri agreed to pay five hundred pounds Egyptian for this translation, and that is why you, Mr Oppenheimer, were not killed by Pappadikos. Instead he makes you work to translate the inscriptions for him.'

Geoff's eyebrows went up. 'You don't say! Sounds like I kinda owe my life to Mr Badri.'

Hadrashi nodded. 'It is so, in a way. I telephone to Cairo today to order the arrest of the Sudanese, and then I telephone Badri and tell him that the tomb, it is found. So—he is here.'

They went to the lounge. Badri was standing beside a palm and smoking an Egyptian cigarette nervously and delicately. His veiled eyes were alive with excitement, and he looked like a man who has found a gold-mine and wants others to know of it but fears to tell them.

He stepped to meet them and shook hands with each of them, making a ceremony of it and bowing. He came to Geoff last and held his hand for so long that the American began to feel embarrassed.

'I am having great pleasure in seeing you,

Mr Oppenheimer,' Badri said in his smooth Egyptian voice. 'When you disappeared I was desolated and I could do nothing.' He smirked. 'But I have great faith in the police of Egypt. I knew they would find you.'

'Without the help of these gentlemen it would be more difficult,' the Colonel said with an odd smile.

Badri released Geoff's hand. 'I have a favour to ask, Mr Oppenheimer. It is the Tomb of Opi. It is many years now that I have been waiting to find this tomb but always I am too busy.' He glanced sideways at Geoff. 'I ask that you show me. Yes?'

Geoff rubbed his head. 'Oh, sure,' he said awkwardly.

Shrimp chuckled. 'I shouldn't think he wants to go within a mile of the place.'

'I'm going back,' Geoff said, 'just as soon as I've seen you two aboard your plane. There's an awful lot of work to be done in that tomb and I don't have much time. Sure, Mr Badri, you can come with me. Glad to have you.'

'You mean you will take me?' Badri said in a small voice, tense with excitement.

Geoff looked puzzled. 'I guess so. That's what I said. Why do you want to go?'

'It is many years since I try to find this tomb. I am interested in Egyptology since I was a boy— but always I must attend to my hotels. Also I am particularly interested in Opi. I think he may be an ancestor of mine. I tell you this before and you cannot believe it, but I would like to know.'

Corrigan grinned incredulously. 'You may be right, Mr Badri, but it's a long time since he died, according to the experts.'

Badri nodded quickly. 'This is true, what you say. But all my life I have a dream from when I am very young. Sometimes I have it and then not again for many months—years perhaps. But it comes again. In this dream I meet a man who tells me that he is Opi, the Chief Priest. He tells me that I am of his line, and that if I will go to his eternal habitation and read there what is written I shall find the proof of this.' He smiled. 'Never have I been able to discover the tomb. Now Mr Oppenheimer will take me to it and read for me the hieroglyphs.'

'Sure,' Geoff said. 'You can work with me. We go to Cairo today so that Corrigan and Shrimp can catch their plane in the morning. Then we come back to Suez and the next day we go to the tomb.'

Badri seized his hand again. 'Always I shall thank you, Mr Oppenheimer. I come with you to Cairo. You stay at my hotel until tomorrow—all of you—free. Please?'

'Very decent of you,' Corrigan murmured. 'In that case Shrimp and I'll go and pack.'

The next morning the big BOAC plane climbed easily out of the desert-heated air of Cairo and into the cooler layers above. As it banked and began to circle the airport, Shrimp and Corrigan could see the tiny squat figures of Geoff, Hadrashi and Badri as they moved towards the Reception Hall.

'The end of another episode,' Shrimp said. 'Now for England, fresh air, cricket and peace.'

Corrigan smiled thoughtfully. He was watching the Delta swing slowly below, an olive-green oasis cut up by roads, canals and the great brooding Nile. Then he saw the sudden start of the desert and, at its edge, the geometrical Pyramids with their triangular shadows, and the old Sphinx gazing for ever towards the Nile, watching and waiting for something unknown.

'We'll come back one day,' Corrigan whispered, 'and see if he's still waiting.' He turned to Shrimp. 'I didn't climb the Great Pyramid after all.'

Shrimp smiled. 'We'll call on our way back to Malaya, so that you can climb it. Or shall we? Wherever we call we seem to collect trouble.'

Printed in Great Britain by
Thomas Nelson and Sons Ltd, Edinburgh